She plopped the pacifier back into the whimpering baby's mouth, lifted up her crier, and took her to the changing table.

Once changed, Callie was happy. Mirela placed her in the baby swing. The continuous giggles and potent aroma coming from Benny's crib meant only one thing.

She scooped the boy up. "Benny, do you have another present for me?"

Louder cackles erupted, and he once again reached for her hair. She nestled her nose into his neck, making him squeal with delight. "You could share a few of these presents with your mommy."

He leaned toward her to plant one of his open-mouthed kisses on her jaw. Mirela couldn't help but adore the little cherub. As she changed the baby, she imagined her son might look like Benny with his dark hair and big brown eyes. Just as she longed to visit Serbia, she also longed for a family. She wanted as many children as the Lord would bless her with. She bit back a chuckle. Of course, she'd have to find a husband first. She was already twenty-five and so far God hadn't brought anyone along. *Not even any prospects.* After washing her hands, she picked Benny up off the changing table. The door opened.

"Are you Mirela Adams?"

Mirela looked up and stared at the tall, dark-haired man. It was her husband.

JENNIFER JOHNSON and her unbelievably supportive husband, Albert, are happily married and raising Brooke, Hayley, and Allie, the three cutest young ladies on the planet. Besides being a middle school teacher, Jennifer loves to read, write, and chauffeur her girls. She is a member of American Christian Fiction Writers. Blessed beyond measure, Jennifer hopes to always think like a child—bigger than imaginable and with complete faith. Send her a note at jenwrites4god@bellsouth.net.

Books by Jennifer Johnson

HEARTSONG PRESENTS
HP725—By His Hand
HP738—Picket Fence Pursuit
HP766—Pursuing the Goal
HP802—In Pursuit of Peace
HP866—Finding Home
HP882—For Better or Worse
HP901—Gaining Love
HP920—Maid to Love
HP938—Betting on Love
HP954—Game of Love

Don't miss out on any of our super romances. Write to us at the following address for information on our newest releases and club information.

Heartsong Presents Readers' Service
PO Box 721
Uhrichsville, OH 44683

Or visit www.heartsongpresents.com

Shoebox Surprise

Jennifer Johnson

Heartsong Presents

This book has been so much fun. The idea was actually one of my favorites that God has given me. Mirela, a woman from Serbia, wrote me several times about how my books blessed her. Her e-mails touched my heart, and I found myself praying often for this woman I have never met. About the same time, our church was collecting items for Operation Christmas Child shoeboxes. One specific woman, Andy Raybourne, feels a true burden for the ministry and leads our church in collecting items throughout the year, just as the heroine does in this book. Put those two things together and a story was born.

Therefore, this book is dedicated to Mirela Crkvenjas and Andy Raybourne. May God use this book to bless others as you two have blessed me.

A note from the Author:
I love to hear from my readers! You may correspond with me by writing:

Jennifer Johnson
Author Relations
PO Box 721
Uhrichsville, OH 44683

Print ISBN 978-1-61626-591-5

eBook Editions:
Adobe Digital Edition (.epub) 978-1-60742-704-9
Kindle and MobiPocket Edition (.prc) 978-1-60742-705-6

SHOEBOX SURPRISE

Scripture taken from the Holy Bible, New International Version®. niv®. Copyright © 1973, 1978, 1984 by International Bible Society. Used by permission of Zondervan. All rights reserved.

This book is a work of fiction. Names, characters, places, and incidents are either products of the author's imagination or used fictitiously.

Our mission is to publish and distribute inspirational products offering exceptional value and biblical encouragement to the masses.

PRINTED IN THE U.S.A.

one

"It is her. I have found her. She is as beautiful as I imagined. Josif, it is your wife."

Josif Sesely twirled the office chair away from the computer screen and gaped at his mother. Her deep-brown eyes peered down at him as she pushed long strands of salt-and-pepper hair behind her ear with one hand, while using the other to shove a newspaper in his face.

"It is Mirela. I am sure of it. She looks like my friend. Her mother. Just like her."

Shaking his head, Josif grabbed the newspaper from his mother's hand and placed it on the desk. "Mama, what are you talking about?"

She lifted both hands in the air and then brought them down and smacked them against her thighs. "Your wife, Josif. Did I not just say this?"

"Mama?"

She leaned over and pointed a dry-skinned finger at an article. Barely a nub of a nail covered the top of her appendage. His mother had worked hard in the modest hotel she and his father purchased in Gatlinburg, Tennessee. Having labored for years to save enough money to journey from Serbia to America, then working just as diligently in the hotel in Gatlinburg they now owned, his mother had never been able to settle down and retire. It didn't matter that Josif's business sense proved quite profitable, allowing both of his parents the ability to enjoy a life of rest. His mother

5

continued to follow the housekeepers, often making it to rooms before they could, to ensure they would be cleaned to her liking. She was never cruel, but she was most certainly particular.

"Mirela." She tapped the photo.

Josif looked at the photo of a dark-haired woman who sat in front of a room full of shoeboxes. The title of the article read PAY IT FORWARD: SHOEBOX MINISTRY. Skimming the caption, he read that the woman in the picture had received a shoebox from a Christian organization when she was a girl living in Serbia. Now, as an American citizen, she and her church put together hundreds of shoeboxes for orphans across the world.

He looked up at his mother. With both excitement and determination, her dark-brown eyes bored into him. He shook his head. "I don't understand what this article has to do with me and my future wife."

She pulled a metal chair closer to him and plopped into it. She pointed to the name of the woman in the picture. "Of course you don't remember. You were such a small boy. This is Mirela."

Josif rubbed his temples. His mother wasn't making sense, and he had a lot of work to do. It was the end of the month, and he needed to be sure the books were properly balanced as well as review the inventory. He didn't have time to read through a paper. He looked at the name at the top of the clipping—it wasn't even a local newspaper. It was from Greenfield, a good forty-five minutes from them. He agreed the hotel should keep copies of newspapers from the surrounding areas available for patrons, but he simply did not have time to read community-interest articles.

"Mama"—he pushed the newspaper toward her—"I have

a lot of work to do. We'll talk about this later. Possibly after dinner."

His mother clucked her tongue and wagged her finger in front of him. "No, son. You will listen now." She inhaled as she shifted in the chair beside him. "Mirela's mother was my closest friend, like my own family. You were a small boy, only five years, when Jovana gave birth to Mirela." She touched his cheek with her hand. "You loved the small babe. Always wanting to touch her head or hold her hand. Her mother and I promised, for we just knew, you and Mirela would be husband and wife one day."

A tear fell down his mother's face, and Josif knew she was thinking back to her life in Knin, the small village on Croatian land. Their Serbian people had lived there peaceably until the Croatians attacked. Ethnic cleansing. His family had moved to America only months before the real slaughtering started. He still remembered his mother's sobs as she watched the happenings on television from the safety of American land.

With the back of her hand, his mother swiped the lone tear away from her cheek. "When my friend was killed and her husband, too, little Mirela went to live with her older sister, and then she was given to another family. . . ." His mother shook her head. "I thought I would never see Jovana's baby again."

"Mama, you do not know—"

She lifted her hand to silence him then pushed the paper back toward him and pointed to the article. "She is from Krajina. It says so right here. You know our town was in that land. The missionaries who adopted her served there." Her mouth widened into a smile he rarely saw so full. Deep   nkles splayed out of the corners of her eyes. Years of hard work in Knin and then at the hotel in Gatlinburg had aged his mother beyond her fifty-five years, but she still had the fight and determination of a woman half her age. "God has allowed us to find her. You must go to Greenfield."

Josif let out a long breath. He had no intention of driving forty-five minutes to search for a woman who looked like his mother's best friend. Even if she did come from their land. It did seem ironic that the woman in the picture's name was Mirela, that she was from Krajina, and that she'd been blessed with Christmas shoeboxes. He remembered his thrill at receiving them more than once. But what were the chances this was the now-grown baby his mother spoke of? It had to be a million to one, or possibly more than that.

"Mama, the chances of this woman being—"

"Unless God has planned this."

He looked up at his mother. The determined gleam in her eyes spoke louder than the logic of the odds of this Mirela being Jovana's daughter. He would be going to Greenfield to find this woman. He'd be embarrassed when she laughed at his mother's ridiculous notion. But he'd go just the same, or he wouldn't know a moment of rest.

❧

Mirela Adams scooped the chubby infant out of the bouncy seat then nuzzled her nose into the crook of his neck. "I think you've produced a stinky little present for me."

Benny cackled and reached for the strands of hair that had escaped her clip. Drool streaked down the right corner of his mouth as he smiled, seeming entirely too pleased with himself. Mirela couldn't hold back a laugh as she placed the seven-month-old baby on the changing table. She glanced at the clock on the wall. She could set her watch by Benny's schedule. Lunch at 11:30. Dirty diaper by noon. He'd made it by five minutes.

His schedule proved quite unhelpful as the two-year-olds were supposed to eat at noon. Not that Mirela should have to worry about that. Cheryl was in charge of the two-year-olds. She should be the one to get them ready to take to the kitchen area for lunch. But what *should* happen usually didn't, and once again Mirela found herself watching her three babies and Cheryl's seven two-year-olds. Supposedly for only five minutes. But that was twenty minutes ago.

She scanned the room quickly to ensure all seven children were playing happily. At any moment someone would break into a chorus of "I'm hungry," and the whole group would follow. She loved the children. Every single one of them. She prayed that one day God would allow her a home full of kids, but ten children ages two and under was more of a challenge than she enjoyed.

She changed Benny's diaper, placed him in the crib, sterilized the changing table, and then washed her hands. Cheryl should return in the next few minutes. Mirela's babies had been fed and were lying in the cribs ready for their naps, and she knew the daycare director, Mrs. Jones, would have the two-year-olds' lunches prepared at twelve sharp.

She clapped the rhythm that meant for the children to stop playing and pay attention. Seven sweet pairs of eyes peered up at her. Mirela noted that blond-haired, blue-eyed Madi was about to start the hunger chorus. Before the child could utter the words, Mirela said, "Let's clean up. It's lunchtime."

Cheers rang through the room as she pushed PLAY on the CD player for the clean-up song. Having made this time much like a game, the two-year-olds thrilled at picking up their toys. She laughed with the children as they tossed blocks into the crate and revved cars into the parking garage.

With the room picked up, Cheryl still hadn't returned. Mirela pushed down the growing irritation in her chest. *It's fish sticks day. Maybe she went to the kitchen to check on Mrs. Jones's progress and discovered lunch was not quite ready.*

Deep in her gut, she knew that wasn't the case. Cheryl left her with the children all too often. Still, Mirela tried to stay positive as she pulled her phone out of her pocket and dialed Cheryl's number. It went straight to voice mail. Her agitation growing, she bit the inside of her lip. One of the day care's rules was always to keep your cell phone on and always to answer. It was a matter of safety.

She knew Cheryl took advantage of her. Mirela was the primary caregiver for the three infants. Cheryl was the primary caregiver for the seven two-year-olds. Because their rooms were joined by a Dutch door, Cheryl suggested they share the burden of the two rooms as often as possible. Initially, Mirela thought the idea a wonderful one. She would be able to take restroom breaks and eat lunch with ease, and she didn't mind watching the two rooms so that Cheryl could do the same. But it hadn't worked out that way. Too often Cheryl went for breaks that took sometimes thirty minutes or longer.

"Me hungry, Miss Mella," red-haired Andy whined.

"Me, too," said another.

Tears welled in Madi's eyes. She was going to be emotional about her hunger. And Mirela didn't blame her. Their schedule was rigid with naptime right after lunch. The children thrived on the routine, and they were already ten minutes past their lunchtime. Her babies were ten minutes into their nap, so she couldn't leave them alone to take the two-year-olds to lunch. Besides, she needed to eat her own lunch while she had the chance.

Unsure what else to do, Mirela dialed Hannah's number. Hannah taught the three-year-olds. With fifteen children in the room, she had a full-time assistant. Hannah's voice sounded over the line. "Hi, Mirela. Let me guess. Cheryl hasn't shown up to take the kiddos to lunch."

Mirela smiled into the phone. Hannah knew the routine as well as Mircla. "How'd you guess that?"

"I can see Cheryl outside my window. She's on her cell phone, having quite the animated discussion with someone."

Mirela sighed. Cheryl fought with her boyfriend. . .a lot. It wasn't Mirela's business, but it really made things difficult at work. Mirela prayed for the woman, that she and her boyfriend would receive Jesus as Lord. For that reason alone, she tried to be patient with her colleague. But she had just about had enough. Regardless, the children had to be cared for.

She heard what sounded like Hannah's pounding on the window. "She's coming. Mirela, you're going to have to have a talk with her, or you're going to have to tell Mrs. Jones."

Mirela let out a long breath. "I know."

She hated confrontation. Hated it more than anything else she could think of. She would rather just do the work than to have to deal with someone else's anger or frustration. She'd seen enough of those emotions in her very young life in Serbia. If it was within her power to keep the peace, she would do it.

Cheryl knew that and took advantage of her.

The door opened, and Cheryl waved the children into the hall. She didn't apologize or say thanks to Mirela, simply ushered the kids to the kitchen area. Mirela bit back the peaked frustration. Hannah was right. Mirela would have to talk with Cheryl, but right now she needed to eat lunch and take care of a few shoebox details while the babies napped.

She pulled a chair beside the window so she could feel the warmth of the sun through the pane. It was a beautiful late-summer day. She would finagle the three babies in the two-child stroller and take them for a walk after naptime. They would enjoy the fresh air as much as she.

After taking a bite of her sandwich, she opened her shoebox journal. Her church had collected combs, tooth-brushes, and toothpaste through the month of August. They were well over their goal of one thousand combs and toothbrushes, but they were 273 tubes short of toothpaste. Using her iPhone, she looked up local dental offices then jotted down their numbers. After work she'd have to call to see if any of them would donate what was needed.

Memories of the shoebox she'd received when she was five flooded her. Having lost her parents when she was only a toddler, she had no memory of them. Mirela's older sister and her husband had taken her in, but Mirela had very few recollections of them either, as she was adopted at six. She did remember sleeping and cuddling with several cousins to ward off the chill of cold nights. And she remembered the shoebox.

Two white men and a woman had driven a truck filled with boxes to their town. At first Mirela hadn't known what to think about their giving each of the children a package. The shoeboxes looked pretty, wrapped in bright colors. But her young mind couldn't wrap itself around the purpose of the pretty box. Until her cousin opened his. The first thing she saw was the bright blue socks and then the toy truck. Amazement filled her.

Then the man handed her a box. Most of the kids were ripping open their gifts, but even as such a small girl, Mirela hadn't wanted to. She wondered if *she'd* have blue socks. They were such a pretty color. A girl beside her opened her box to find a doll with yellow hair. Mirela almost squealed with aching for a yellow-haired doll.

Finally she gently opened her box. So many wonderful things filled it. A comb for her hair. Toothpaste. Toothbrush. Pink socks, so much prettier than her cousin's blue ones. Crayons and coloring books, peppermints, and ribbons for her hair. And the doll.

She'd named the doll Carol, after the woman who had brought the shoebox. It was the most beautiful doll she'd ever seen. With dark-brown hair and bright green eyes, she was soft all over. She wore a green, plaid dress and green shoes that were stitched to her body. She was perfect. Soft enough to cuddle. Small enough to smash into bed between Mirela and her cousins.

Baby Carol became her constant companion. When Mirela was adopted at age six, Carol went with her. When she and her new family moved to America, Carol did as well. When her precious adopted father passed away, Carol was there. Even now, at age twenty-five, Mirela still kept Carol on her bed.

Mirela ate the last bite of her sandwich then closed her journal. After placing it back in the GOD IS LOVE tote bag her sister bought her for her last birthday, she peered out the window. The playground was filled with the class of four-year-olds. Looking past them, Mirela stared at the mountains in the distance. She loved Tennessee. Loved hiking and camping with her adopted sister. She looked forward to the hiking trip they were planning.

And yet, a piece of her still longed for Serbia, although she didn't want to live there. Tennessee was her home. She didn't feel God calling her into full-time missions. But she yearned to take shoeboxes to her native land, to see the delighted looks on the children's faces, and to have the opportunity to share Jesus with them. And this year, she might actually get to go.

She closed her eyes. *God, You know my heart. You know my desire.*

A whimper sounded from across the room. A cry followed quickly and then cackles from Benny. The babies woke up the same way each day, and almost always the moment she started to pray. She shook her head and smiled. "Guess we'll talk about this later, Lord."

She plopped the pacifier back into the whimpering baby's mouth, lifted up her crier, and took her to the changing table. Once changed, Callie was happy. Mirela placed her in the baby swing. The continuous giggles and potent aroma coming from Benny's crib meant only one thing.

She scooped the boy up. "Benny, do you have another present for me?"

Louder cackles erupted, and he once again reached for her hair. She nestled her nose into his neck, making him squeal with delight. "You could share a few of these presents with your mommy."

He leaned toward her to plant one of his open-mouthed kisses on her jaw. Mirela couldn't help but adore the little cherub. As she changed the baby, she imagined her son might look like Benny with his dark hair and big brown eyes. Just as she longed to visit Serbia, she also longed for a family. She wanted as many children as the Lord would bless her with. She bit back a chuckle. Of course, she'd have to find a husband first. She was already twenty-five and so far God hadn't brought anyone along. *Not even any prospects.* After washing her hands, she picked Benny up off the changing table. The door opened.

"Are you Mirela Adams?"

Mirela looked up and stared at the tall, dark-haired man. It was her husband.

two

Mirela shook her head. What was she thinking? Caring for Benny was obviously putting ridiculous, fanciful notions in her head. Who in her right mind saw a man for the first time in her life and decided he was the man for her? The man she would marry? She inwardly chuckled at the foolish notion. She was tired. That was all.

And yet, she couldn't deny the man was quite handsome—thick, dark hair; deep-brown eyes with flecks of hazel. He had a strong jawline and straight white teeth. He was taller than most of the men she knew, and the girth of his shoulders and chest was apparent beneath his deep-green polo shirt. The hint of a Serbian accent caused a deep stirring she'd never before known.

Benny grabbed her small hoop earring, forcing her back to reality. She pulled the baby's hand away from her ear. "No. No."

The man still stood just inside the doorway, waiting for her response. She swallowed. Probably he was the father of a newborn and wanted a tour of the facility. Although that didn't seem likely because the daycare director usually scheduled and then guided tours, and Mirela hadn't been notified of one today.

Her gaze traveled to his left hand. He wore no wedding band. But that meant very little. Many of the children came from single-parent homes. Forcing a smile to her lips, she nodded. "I am Mirela Adams. This is the infant room."

Holding Benny tight on her hip, she swept her free hand across the room. "As you can see, we have three babies at present. We are certified to care for five at one time. How old is your child?"

The man scrunched his nose and took a step back. "I don't have a baby. I'm not even married."

Mirela tightened her hold on Benny and took a step toward the other children. The man appeared nice enough, like he was an everyday, average kind of guy. But one could never tell. And who had let him in anyway? The doors were locked. Mrs. Jones only allowed in parents or occasionally family members of the workers who needed to drop something off. One of the babies started to fuss, and Mirela placed the pacifier back in the infant's mouth. She'd hoped to take them for a walk before the next feeding time, but it didn't appear that would happen.

Feeling very protective, she stared at the man. "How may I help you, sir?"

He clasped his hands then rubbed them together. She noticed a slight pink tinge of color streaking up his neck. He cleared his throat. "You said you're Mirela Adams, right?"

She straightened. "I am."

He shoved his hands into his jeans pockets, swallowed, then said, "Have you ever heard of the name Slobodon?"

She stiffened and her heart seemed to skip a beat in her chest. "Yes. I know the name."

A shadow of relief seemed to spread across his features and he nodded. "Was it your name?"

Curiosity and excitement washed over her. How would this man know her name? Did he know something of her past? She longed to know her family, to know that they served God. She yearned to know more about the parents she could never see this side of heaven. If she could only know they were Christians, that they'd received Jesus. She'd spent many nights praying they were. And her sister who'd taken her in when Mirela was barely older than Benny. She remembered so little of the woman and her cousins, but she longed to share Christ with them.

A moment of hesitation weeded through her before she could answer his question. Who was this man? What did he know or want to know about her birth family? As quickly as the questions filled her mind, God's peace flooded her soul. He was in charge of her life and her past and all who knew her past. She looked into the man's eyes and nodded. "Yes. That was my name."

The man's jaw dropped and his eyes widened in surprise. "You're kidding?"

Something about the complete disbelief that wrapped his features made Mirela giggle. She shook her head. "Not kidding."

"I can't believe it." The man scratched his jaw. He pulled a newspaper clipping from his back pocket. Mirela recognized it as the article about her that had recently appeared in the *Greenfield Gazette*.

Curiosity swelled within her. No longer feeling any danger, she pointed toward a chair. "If you'd like to have a seat, I'll warm the babies' bottles, and then we'll talk."

The man sat down. After warming the milk, she propped up the bottles for the boys to eat and nestled Callie into her arms. It was her turn to be cuddled while she ate. The man focused on the article as if it was the first time he'd actually read it. "May I ask your name, sir?"

He looked at her. Disbelief still covered his face. "Of course." He refolded the article. "I am Josif Sesely. My family is from Krajina." He pointed at Callie. "Apparently I've known you since you were her age."

❧

Excitement washed across her features. "Are you my brother or one of my cousins?"

"No." Josif waved his hands in front of him. He bit back a chuckle as he thought of his mother's adamancy that he and Mirela were destined for matrimony. Being her brother or cousin might make that a bit of a challenge.

"Then how do you know me?"

"My mother and your mother were best friends in Knin, the town where we lived. My mother told me you were a small girl when your parents died." He scratched at the stubble on his jaw. He wished he'd paid better attention to what his mother had said about Mirela Slobodon. But he hadn't believed it could possibly be her. What were the chances that his mother's best friend's daughter from Serbia would live only forty-five minutes away from them in Tennessee? The odds seemed insurmountable.

"Unless God has planned this." His mother's continuous, annoying comment over the last few days slipped into his mind. He'd come only to appease her. To stop her nagging. And she'd been right.

He watched as Mirela lifted the baby over her shoulder and burped her. In one deft movement, she laid the girl down and picked up a boy to burp him as well. She was good with the infants. Her quick, gentle movements mesmerized him and stirred something within his stomach.

As his mother often reminded him, he knew it was nearing time to settle down. At thirty, not only had he reached an age where he wanted to begin a family, but the hotel was also established and financially sound. He imagined Mirela would make a wonderful mother.

What was he thinking? He'd been dating Sabrina for three years. She was beautiful and, as the manager of the nationwide chain coffee shop in his hotel, she was a terrific business partner—frugal and precise, yet able to keep the customers happy. She was the kind of woman he'd always intended to marry.

He wasn't sure he could envision her holding a baby as gingerly as Mirela had, but she could learn. She would learn when the babe was her own. Sabrina would be every bit as nurturing. And if she wasn't, at least the child would be raised with a good business sense. He would be able to take over the family business with ease.

Josif shook his head. Each thought grew more disturbing and didn't serve the purpose of his visit with Mirela.

A woman opened the top half of the Dutch door. "Hey, Mirela, I need your help for a minute." She turned her head and noticed him. "Oh. I didn't know we could have friends over while we worked."

The woman's tone grated on his nerves, and he found himself wanting to defend Mirela.

"What do you need, Cheryl?" Mirela asked.

"I need you to watch the kids for a minute."

Josif watched Mirela let out a long breath. He wondered if the woman needed Mirela's help a lot.

"Give me five minutes."

The woman sighed and shut the top door with a smack.

Mirela turned back to him. "I would really like to talk with you." She brushed a loose strand of hair away from her cheek. "I've always wanted to know more about my family."

"Could I meet you after work?" The words slipped out before he'd had a chance to think them through. She probably didn't get off work for at least another two hours. What would he do until then? Drive around the delightfully small town of Greenfield? Still he did want to talk with Mirela, this person from his past, from another world entirely.

"We could meet at Bo's Diner at six o'clock. Would that work for you?"

He glanced at his wristwatch. That gave him three hours to kill. "Sounds great." He stood then walked toward the door.

"Do you need directions?"

He swatted his hand. "I've got plenty of time to find it."

As he headed toward the front door of the facility, he waved at the director. "See you next weekend."

"You sure will. Thanks, Mr. Sesely."

He'd had to show his identification, wait while she checked for his name on some criminal site, and promise the woman a free night's stay at the hotel in order to go back and talk with Mirela—the woman his mother had suspected her of being. He couldn't deny his excitement to talk more with her. He pulled his cell phone out of his pocket. But first he'd have to find out more information from his mother.

three

As usual, Benny's mother, Emily, was the last to pick up her son. Mirela waved at Bella, the six-year-old girl, strapped into the backseat. "Do you still want me to pick them up tomorrow night for church?"

Emily smiled. "That would be wonderful. It will give me a chance to get some laundry done."

Mirela's heart broke for the poor woman. She'd been crushed when her husband left without a word right after Benny's birth. They received no assistance from the father, and Mirela tried to help whenever she could. And though she hadn't yet been able to persuade the young mother to attend church with her, she was able to see that Benny and his sister were in church every Sunday and Wednesday.

"No problem." Mirela kissed the top of Benny's head and handed him and the diaper bag to his mother. "See you tomorrow, big boy."

Going back into the day care facility, she hoped for time to run by the house to change her clothes. A quick glance at the clock let her know that wasn't a possibility. She looked at the spit-up stuck to her left shoulder. It smelled every bit as awful as it appeared.

She texted her mom and sister to let them know she wouldn't be home for dinner then walked into the bathroom, knowing she had to freshen up, even if just a bit. Grabbing several paper towels out of the dispenser, she wetted and soaped them up then tackled the stain on her shoulder. By the time she finished, the spot was wet and bigger, but at least it no longer smelled.

She unclipped her hair and then pulled a brush out of her purse. Brushing through her long, thick locks was always a chore, but she knew her hair was her greatest physical feature. She wished she had some makeup in her purse. Mascara or blush at least, but all she had was lip gloss. Applying a coat to her mouth, she smacked her lips together. Studying herself in the mirror, she shrugged. It was the best she could do. "It's not like people get all dressed up to eat at Bo's."

She shoved the items back into her purse. It wasn't as if she needed to look pretty anyway. Not that she was interested in the man. She'd only met him three hours ago.

An image of his deep-brown eyes flashed through her mind, and she smiled at her reflection. "But I can't deny he is cute."

"You're not kidding about that, honey—that is if you're talking about the hunk who came to see you this afternoon."

Mirela's face heated as her boss walked out of the stall at the far end of the restroom. The woman laughed. "Don't look so guilty. There's nothing wrong with you thinking the man is good looking. You're a single woman."

"Yes, ma'am."

Mrs. Jones turned on the faucet then bumped her hip against Mirela. "Don't you 'yes, ma'am' me. Makes me feel old. You just have fun with that fellow."

Trying to hold her humiliation at bay, Mirela nodded, grabbed her purse, and walked out of the bathroom. Making her way to her car, she searched her mind for memories of Serbia. Josif said he'd known her parents. But her parents died when she was barely over a year old. There was no way she would be able to conjure memories of him and his family.

After unlocking her car, she slipped inside and started the engine. She wondered if she looked like her mother or father. Her adopted sister, Ivy, had beautiful blond hair and blue eyes. She was the spitting image of her mother. Mirela wondered if her biological mother had the single dimple in her left cheek as Mirela did, or if maybe her father had it. Or maybe neither. Or both. She had so many questions. So many things she wanted to know.

Pulling into the parking lot of the diner, her heart began to beat violently in her chest. Questions raced through her mind, things she hoped he could answer. If she was honest, she'd admit part of the trepidation came from her attraction to him.

She took several deep breaths as she made her way into the restaurant. She spied him in the back corner. Although he hadn't noticed her yet, she continued to walk toward him. When he looked up, the smile spreading across his face made her toes curl inside her tennis shoes. The man was entirely too cute.

A sudden wave of shyness washed over her, and heat flooded her neck and cheeks. "Hello, again."

He held up his phone. "I spent two hours on the phone with my mother. She is beside herself that you are Mirela Sobodon. She believes God has brought you back into her life."

Peace wrapped itself around her. "I believe God can do absolutely anything."

"Even bring together two families from Serbia?"

"Even that."

Josif studied her for several moments. Normally she would begin to fidget under such intensive scrutiny, but she felt as if God had wrapped His arms around her, offering her a gift she didn't even know how to ask for.

Josif nodded slowly. "I believe that as well."

God, what is going on? What are You doing? When I woke up this morning, I never would have dreamed I would meet a man who knew me from Serbia. And he's a Christian!

Mirela's heart filled with such joy she feared it would burst into a zillion pieces. Though not biologically related to her adopted father, she shared the burning he'd had for the Serbian people—that they would know Jesus and His resurrection and His love. They were her people, her family. And here sat a man from her homeland, who knew Jesus. She shifted in her seat to keep the *hallelujah* from springing out of her mouth.

"So, what can I get you to drink, sweetie?"

Mirela looked up at the waitress. She didn't know the woman personally, but she'd seen her several times. "Sweet tea."

"Lemon?"

"No thank you."

"Okay. Be right back to take your orders."

The woman shuffled away, favoring her right leg. Mirela wondered if she had arthritis, as she walked so much like her adopted mother who struggled with it. Josif pointed to his glass. "I'm addicted to the stuff myself."

She smiled. "So, tell me about my family. And yours."

❧

Josif drank in the animation on her features. She seemed to mentally churn every word he said, sifting through it, obviously longing for memories to form. Mirela was much more beautiful than her picture in the newspaper. He hadn't realized earlier in the day how long and thick her hair was. She had pulled the mass across her left shoulder. It fell in soft curls almost to her stomach. His fingers itched to touch it, to see if it was as soft as it looked.

"Tell me about your mother," she said as she forked up some mashed potatoes.

"She's dying to meet you. I can tell you that."

Mirela's lips parted into a smile that lit up the room. "I would like to meet her as well."

Josif leaned back in the booth. The restaurant was more crowded than he would have expected for a weekday, but he had to admit he enjoyed the atmosphere. Though Bo's Diner looked like a metal building from the outside, the inside was designed to look like an open log cabin. Dark wood lined the walls and ceiling. Wood beams supported the roof in various places. Lantern-shaped lights hung along the walls, and antler chandeliers suspended down from above the booths. In the center of the room were several wooden tables as well as a salad bar.

And the food was delicious. His steak was tender, and the mashed potatoes practically melted in his mouth. Mirela hadn't finished her fried chicken, and Josif had to hold back the urge to ask if he could sample it.

"We'll have to arrange it." He leaned forward and clasped his hands on top of the table. "In fact, if you don't tell me a few things about yourself before I leave, my mother will never forgive me."

Mirela laughed, a soft, sweet sound, and Josif wished he could say something else so he could hear it again. She reached for her purse. "I have a few pictures."

He raised his eyebrows. "I'd love to see them."

She sifted through her wallet then handed him a picture of her and a blond-haired woman. "This is my sister, Ivy. It was one of our college graduation pictures."

Josif studied the photo of Mirela and her sister. They were facing each other in an embrace. Both looked as if they'd been blessed with the greatest of treasures—each other. "You two are close?"

"Very close. Same age even. She is my best friend in the whole world. I would do anything for her."

"Where did the two of you go to school?"

"We started at Walter State, then transferred to UT. We both have degrees in education. She teaches elementary, but my degree is in early childhood."

"I graduated from the University of Tennessee as well. Business."

She pumped her fist. "Go Vols." It was the quietest show of support for UT's Volunteers that he'd ever witnessed, and he couldn't hold back a chuckle.

She continued. "I'm a huge Tennessee football fan. Love my Peyton Manning. Even became an Indianapolis Colts fan because of him."

His mouth dropped. He knew it did. He could feel it. She was a woman after his own heart. "Football? Really? I've got two season tickets to UT's games."

She reached across the table and placed her hand on his arm. Her eyes blazed with excitement. "No, you do not."

He nodded. "Yes, I do."

"I haven't been to a game since I graduated."

"Well, maybe we could go."

She started to nod, then she swallowed, pulled her hand away, and leaned back in the booth. A slight blush covered her cheeks. "Sorry about that. I get a little excited about my Vols."

Josif shrugged. "I completely understand."

His phone vibrated in his front pocket. The country song

Sabrina had put into his phone pelted through the room. He didn't really like the ringtone, and it annoyed him every time he heard it. Pushing the TALK button, he lifted the phone to his ear. "Hello, Sabrina."

"You said you'd be home for dinner."

His girlfriend's whine sounded through the phone at such a decibel that he knew Mirela could hear her. He noticed she twisted her napkin in her hands. She looked around the room, obviously trying not to listen to the conversation.

"I'm sorry, Sabrina. The visit was a little longer than I expected. But Mirela is who my mother thought."

"So." He didn't have to see Sabrina in person to picture her bottom lip stuck out in a pout. She'd been acting funny the last few days. He wondered if she'd heard his mother mention the ridiculous notion that he and Mirela were destined for each other. The idea was a crazy one, but he and Sabrina had been a couple long enough that she shouldn't be worried about such things.

"I'll be leaving in a few minutes."

"You better. I'm tired of waiting."

The line clicked off before he had the chance to respond. He didn't appreciate Sabrina's tone, and what did she mean by "I'm tired of waiting"? How many times in their relationship had he waited for her? She was late for dates, canceled often because of business, and she had been the one for the first two years of the relationship who was determined to keep business first, love second.

"I've kept you too long. I'd better let you get going." Mirela pulled several bills out of her purse.

Josif held back a growl at the apology in her tone. He pushed the money back at her. "Oh no. I'm buying your dinner."

She didn't argue, just put the money in her purse and stood. She took a step away from him. *Is she going to leave without so much as a good-bye?* His mother would never let him hear the end of it.

"Wait a minute." He slid out of the booth and grabbed her arm. "We have to plan our next meeting."

She furrowed her brows. "I. . .uh. . ."

"How about you come to the hotel this Saturday? Mama will be very upset with me if I don't get you two together soon."

"Well, I'm not. . ."

He peered into her eyes. Something about her drew him in a way he'd not experienced before. She felt like home. "Please."

She seemed to battle the suggestion in her mind. After a slight sigh, she nodded. "Okay."

He grabbed a business card out of his wallet and handed it to her. "If you need any help with directions. . ."

She shook her head. "I have a GPS in my car."

"Good." He smiled then without thinking pushed a strand of hair away from her cheek. Her eyes widened, and he felt his face warm. He cleared his throat. "If I didn't set up a date for you to meet my mother, she'd never again allow me back in her house."

four

As Ivy pulled one item after another out of the donated bag, Mirela added the names of the gifts to her laptop's computer program she used for the shoebox ministry. She and her adopted family had put together Christmas shoeboxes since the first year they'd returned to the States from their decade of work in the Serbian mission field. Each year Mirela's burden for the ministry grew. Ivy and her mother had always been supportive, and this year the goal was to send one thousand shoeboxes to countries around the world.

Mirela looked around the unfinished basement. Toiletries, small garments, toys, stuffed animals, and gadgets filled half of the room. That didn't include the seven hundred empty shoeboxes lining the far right wall.

"Every year I'm amazed at how many items we collect for the shoeboxes." Ivy stood and placed a small doll in the refrigerator box already filled to the top with an assortment of stuffed animals.

"Every year I remember how much my shoebox meant to me."

Mirela thought of her Christmases since being adopted. She and her sister woke up to presents spilling out from underneath their artificial evergreen. She remembered the first time they'd hung glowing white lights and shiny, red balls on the tree. It was the most beautiful thing she'd ever seen. She'd thought that was her present for that year. Waking up Christmas morning to brightly colored gifts that she was able to unwrap and then enjoy—it was more than her young heart knew how to handle. She'd spent much of the afternoon in tears, unsure how to cope with it all.

Ivy grabbed Mirela's hand and squeezed. "I'm so glad God gave me a sister."

Mirela raised her eyebrows. "What about when I borrowed your white sweater and then spilled chocolate syrup on it?"

Ivy wrinkled her nose. "Except then." She cocked her head. "I believe I got you back when I used your hairbrush on the dog."

Mirela shook her head. "I still can't believe you did that."

Ivy laughed. Her blue eyes sparkled with merriment. "I thought Mom would strangle me."

"If Dad hadn't laughed at your antics, she might have."

Mirela closed the laptop, set it on the folding table, then sat in a lawn chair. She needed to tell Ivy about Josif and his family, but what should she say? Possibly just blurt out his visit to the day care. It still seemed surreal to her, as if she would wake up at any moment from a dream. Then she would look at the business card he'd given her and know he had not been a figment of her imagination. She bit the inside of her lip, pondering her words.

"What's going on, Mel?"

Mirela smiled at the nickname Ivy had given her soon after she'd been adopted. Ivy only used it when they needed to discuss something serious. Mirela scratched her eyebrow then twirled a strand of hair around her finger.

"Uh-oh. This is serious. You're twirling." Ivy pulled a lawn chair up beside her and plopped into it. "Spit it out."

Mirela shivered. The basement was naturally cooler than the rest of the house, but she couldn't tell if the involuntary motion originated from the temperature or her nerves. Either way, she had to fess up to her sister. "I'm going to Gatlinburg tomorrow."

Ivy furrowed her eyebrows and sat back in the chair. "Okay. . . ?" She twisted in the seat. "Doing a little shopping?"

"Not exactly. I'm going to meet a woman who says she was my mother's best friend."

"Frannie Mitchell?" Ivy sat up and clasped her hands. "Mom will be thrilled. I didn't know she and her husband had begun their furlough from Japan."

Mirela pointed from herself to Ivy. "Not *our* mother's best friend." She pointed back at her chest. "*My* mother's best friend."

Ivy's mouth formed a perfect O as confusion wrapped her expression. "But how did you meet?" She placed her index finger on her lip then opened her hands in front of her. "Well, I guess you haven't met. . .but how did you hear of her?"

In a gust of emotion, Mirela shared about Josif Sesely and his showing up at the day care a few days before. She talked about their dinner and how the man seemed to know so many details of her life. Even if Mirela couldn't remember most of them, they made sense in regard to the geography of where she'd come from and the time he spoke of. "He knew my name before Adams."

"Okay." Ivy's features remained crinkled as she contemplated the situation. "But does that mean you should believe this man. What was his name again?"

"Josif Sesely."

"And they own a hotel?"

Mirela nodded. "Gatlinburg Getaway Hotel."

"And you'll meet in a public place?"

"The lobby of the hotel."

"What did he look like?"

Absolutely gorgeous. Dark-brown hair. Deep-brown eyes with the slightest flecks of hazel. Strong features. Broad shoulders. Mirela shook the description away. "He was Serbian, in appearance and accent."

"But how do you know he is who he says he is?"

Mirela reopened the laptop and clicked on the website to his hotel. She'd visited the site at least a hundred times since his surprise visit. She hadn't found any pictures of a woman who would be old enough to be Josif's mother, but she had found him, as well as a woman who appeared to be his sister. She pointed to the screen. "This is him." She pulled out of her back jeans pocket the frayed business card he'd given her. "This is his card. It matches the hotel and his name."

Ivy elbowed Mirela in the ribs and winked. "He's cute."

Mirela felt her face warm, and Ivy burst into chortles. "I see you think so, too."

"Ivy, I'm being serious." She turned toward her sister. Ivy was a true beauty. Clear, pale skin. Light-blue eyes. Soft blond hair. She was a younger version of their mother. Mirela had never been jealous of the comments Ivy and their mother received about being mirror images, but she'd still longed to know more about where she'd come from. She grabbed her sister's hand. "I've been praying about it constantly since he showed up at the day care. It's something I feel I've got to do."

Ivy squeezed her grip. "Okay. Maybe I could come with you."

Their mother appeared on the bottom step. "Or maybe you shouldn't go at all."

❧

Josif watched as Sabrina prepared a cappuccino and a black coffee for a middle-aged woman. He'd been unable to focus on his work. His continuous thoughts, as well as his mother's consistent interruptions about Mirela's visit the following day, made it impossible to get any work accomplished. He finally gave up and made his way to the lobby a bit early for his and Sabrina's dinner date.

He could never deny Sabrina was a vision of loveliness. She wore her dark, straight hair in long, choppy layers that glistened in the light. Big brown eyes were framed with the longest eyelashes he'd ever seen. They practically swept across her cheek each time she blinked. High cheekbones. Full, pink lips and a pearly white smile. Sabrina could grace the cover of any magazine without digital image editing, and every woman in America would be envious.

Mirela, for example, wasn't nearly as striking as Sabrina. Her hair was beautiful, longer and wavy, but it lacked Sabrina's shine. Her eyes, though close to the same color, were nowhere near as big. He hadn't noticed her eyelashes, though her cheekbones were high and her teeth straight, and her lips had been quite mesmerizing a couple of times when she spoke to him. He pulled at his collar and stretched his neck. *Josif, get a grip.*

Sabrina glanced his way and spied him staring at her. She winked at him, evoking a smile. He walked toward her as she gave the woman her change. Sabrina touched the woman's sleeve. "That blue blouse looks beautiful on you. It brings out the light color of your eyes."

"Thank you, dear." The woman's grin lit up her face as she placed her change in the tips cup.

The woman walked away, and Sabrina leaned over the counter and planted a quick kiss on his cheek. She nodded toward the woman. " 'Course, she's probably a decade or two too old to wear those shoes." Sabrina rolled her eyes. "I don't know what some women are thinking."

Josif's chest tightened. Sabrina had little quips about many of the people they saw when they were together. Normally he ignored her slights, since she didn't say them to anyone but him. But today, for some reason, it bothered him that she often had a negative comment about almost everyone they encountered. Even after she'd just complimented the person. He looked at his own shoes. He wondered what she really thought about him.

She untied her apron and patted his arm. "Let me go get my bag and tell Amber I'm heading out, then I'll be ready."

Josif turned and leaned his back against the counter. He spotted the woman sitting at a small table across from a man who was probably her husband. Her shoes didn't look all that awful to Josif. Just girly, black shoes. The heel was a little high. Probably not very comfortable for walking around Gatlinburg, but for all he knew the couple may be heading to the Titanic Museum or the Dixie Stampede.

He looked around the lobby, trying to envision the place as if he were a patron who'd just walked in. He had adamantly protested the new decor his mother and sister had selected. He'd been convinced they should paint with neutral colors and purchase browns and greens for furniture and rugs.

But he had lost the battle when his father took the women's side. The walls were neutral, but instead of carpet, the lobby sported large white tile with smaller black tile accents. Deep-green and burnt-red rugs and furnishings filled the room, along with oversized artificial plants and abstract art. He had to admit it looked clean and modern, yet felt comfortable and soothing. Most importantly, it looked different than most of the hotels in Gatlinburg.

The reviews they'd received since the redecorating had all been positive. The hotel was already known for its courteous staff. He reveled at the idea that people would appreciate the appearance as well.

His sister, Sofija, walked through the front door, followed by his niece, Chloe, and nephews, Ross and Cole. Josif waved at them. His sister's eyebrows rose when she saw him. The two boys marched past him with barely a nod, no doubt heading to the arcade where his father, their *deda*, had given them free access to all the games.

Sofija wrapped her arms around him. "Hello, little brother." She never failed in greeting him the same way. "Mama is beside herself about Mirela's visit tomorrow. Papa asked me to come over to keep her occupied tonight." She pointed to the oversize bag hanging from her shoulder. "I've brought Phase 10 and Yahtzee."

Josif chuckled. His mother was hooked on the games. She constantly begged him and his father to play, but both of them detested spending time on such mindless activities. Or maybe it was just that she beat them every time.

His sister pointed to her five-year-old daughter. "Chloe is going through some kind of cowgirl stage. She was determined to wear those boots over here." Sofija shrugged. "I figured, what would it hurt for her to come to her grandparents' apartment in a jumpsuit and cowboy boots?"

Several years ago, his parents had renovated four joined rooms into an apartment on the first floor of the hotel. It allowed them to always be available if a need ever arose.

Chloe lifted her right foot in the air. "Deda bought them for me."

Sofija leaned closer to Josif. "And I may never forgive Papa for it."

Josif laughed then bent down to examine his niece's boots. "They look pretty special to me. I bet you're the only girl

Deda bought boots like that for."

Chloe grinned and batted her eyelashes up at her mother. Sofija was fighting a losing battle with the child. His parents spoiled the children in excess, wanting to give them all the things they hadn't been able give Josif and Sofija when they were younger. On several occasions, Sofija's husband had pointedly denied his in-laws' buying one trinket or another for their grandchildren.

Sabrina walked out from the back of the shop. She smiled at them. "I'm ready, Josif." She nodded to his sister and niece.

"Is Josif taking you to dinner?"

"Yes."

Sofija winked at him. "I'm glad to hear that. My brother works too hard."

Sabrina quipped. "Someone does have to look over the hotel's finances."

Josif furrowed his eyebrows. It was an innocent enough statement, but the tone in Sabrina's voice belied something more—an air of authority or superiority. Did she always talk to his family in that way?

Chloe pulled on Sabrina's arm. "Look at my boots, Sabrina. Aren't they pretty?"

A full smile spread his girlfriend's lips as she leaned down to Chloe's level. "They are absolutely adorable. And you're wearing them with a jumpsuit."

She laughed and tickled Chloe's stomach. Josif couldn't help but glance at the middle-aged couple sitting at the small table. Sabrina had been callous about the woman's shoes. Surely, she wouldn't think such things about a five-year-old's wardrobe choice.

He studied his girlfriend for several moments. She probably wouldn't think less of Chloe, but she might of his sister. He watched as the two women talked. Sofija wasn't herself around Sabrina. She was tamer, a bit more cautious with her words. The realization punched him hard in the stomach.

His sister hefted the bag higher on her shoulder. "Chloe and I better get going. I've brought games to keep Mama from fretting over seeing Mirela tomorrow. Have fun."

Josif took Sabrina's arm and guided her out of the hotel.

Sabrina stiffened. "If I hear one more word about Mirela Slobodon. . ."

He leaned down to be sure he heard Sabrina correctly. "What did you say?"

She flashed him a smile that lit up the room. "Nothing." She snuggled closer to him. "Let's just enjoy our evening."

That had been his plan, but already he felt a little sick to his stomach.

five

Josif carried the cake his mother had baked for Mirela into one of the conference rooms. His mother and sister had spent several hours decorating the room with pink and brown polka dot crepe paper and balloons. He placed the confection on the pink tablecloth. *Welcome Mirela* was written in cursive on it. Then he noted that the plates, napkins, and cups matched the decorations. He'd told his mother that Mirela seemed shy, and that a party of this sort might overwhelm her. But Mama hadn't listened.

His mother held her Serbian scrapbook in her hands. He'd looked through it hundreds of times. There were few pictures of their family, as cameras were not commonplace when they lived in Krajina, but Mama had kept all the clippings she could find over the years regarding Serbia. She also held a journal she'd started several days ago. Actually, Sofija had done all the writing. His mother spoke English clearly enough, but she struggled with the writing. Still, Mama wanted to share memories of Mirela's mother, Jovana. Remembering the gleam in Mirela's eyes when he'd shared what little he knew of her family, he smiled knowing she would be thrilled with the journal.

"She should be here any minute." His mother grasped his arm and squeezed. "I can hardly wait, son."

Josif kissed his mother's head. She was the kindest of all people, and he prayed Mirela would appreciate all the work she'd put into their meeting.

He spotted Sabrina across the room. He hadn't seen her come in. She looked breathtaking in her black dress and silver heels. He frowned. She was a bit overdressed for the occasion. His mom and sister wore some kind of short pants. He couldn't remember what they called them. They were nicer than shorts, but nowhere near as fancy as a dress.

She spied him, and with a heavy heart he made his way toward her. He hadn't enjoyed their dinner the night before. Her snide comments seemed to fall one on top of the other, and he wasn't sure what to think about them. Surely she had not changed in less than a week's time. He knew he'd been busy making the hotel all his parents dreamed it could be, but he couldn't imagine he'd been dating such a heartless woman for three years. And not even realized it.

God, what does this say about her faith? What does it say about mine?

Possibly he was simply tired. He'd put in a lot of hours over the last several months. With the renovations complete, things were settling down, and he was learning to adjust to a more administrative role. And possibly Sabrina was a bit tense about meeting Mirela. His mother had certainly made a big deal about the woman.

He let out a long breath as he reached his girlfriend then bent down to give her a slight kiss on the cheek. She grabbed his hand in hers and smiled up at him as if he were the only man she'd ever seen before. Yes, his worry stemmed from mere fatigue. Everything was just fine.

❧

Mirela tried to focus on the signs that led to Gatlinburg, but the argument she'd had with her mother the evening before kept replaying through her mind.

"Why would you want to meet those people?" her mother

bellowed when Mirela told her all Josif had shared.

"Mom, I just want to know about my past," Mirela responded.

"You don't know those people. Just because he said he was a Christian doesn't mean it's true. It could be a trap," her mother wailed.

She and Ivy tried to calm her. Most of what she said didn't even make sense. She'd ranted about giving Mirela everything she could ever want, about being a good mother to her. She tried to talk with her mother, tried to get her to understand how much she longed to know more about her heritage. But she wouldn't hear any part of it. And Mirela hadn't known what to say or do.

She loved her mom. She was the only mom she'd ever known, and she'd been more wonderful than any she could have imagined. It hurt her to think she'd upset her mother.

But God, I have to know. I have to do this.

Peace wrapped itself around her, and she knew God blessed her trip, and that He would comfort her mom.

Determined to shift her thoughts, she focused on the road. The parkway grew more congested as she drove deeper into the city of Gatlinburg. She watched for signs of the Gatlinburg Getaway Hotel, but traffic had slowed to a near crawl. She assumed many of the visitors were enjoying their last few weekends of August.

She passed the Ripley's Believe It or Not Museum with its cracked walls. She'd never gone on a tour. The place weirded her out, although she had to admit she wanted to see the two-headed calf the place boasted having. A giggle swelled within her when she drove by the Hollywood Star Cars Museum. Her dad would have loved to see General Lee from *The Dukes of Hazzard*. She spied the sky lift just ahead.

She'd always wanted to take a ride over the mountains, to see them from an aerial view. Living less than an hour from the tourist area, she should have done so already, but she rarely traveled to the Gatlinburg area.

Her heart sped up when she saw her destination on the left. The hotel was larger than she expected. It was a rectangular, all brown stone structure. The railings, windows, and doorframes were trimmed a dark green, the same shade as the metal roof. A pond and small trees and bushes adorned a small green area in the front. She could see a patio along the side that she assumed was the pool area. She felt an odd sense of pride that it appeared well kept.

Swallowing back her trepidation, she parked toward the back of the parking lot. She needed a moment to collect herself, and she didn't want to risk anyone seeing her. She pulled down the visor and studied her reflection. Her makeup still looked fine, except her lips. She pulled out a tube of lipstick and reapplied the light shade. She put her tresses in a side ponytail, allowing the mass of her hair to fall down her right shoulder. She peered down at her light green capris. The drive had been long enough to ensure they would be wrinkled once she stood up, but at least her white eyelet, button-up blouse should be fine.

The butterflies in her stomach seemed to go to battle, and she felt bile rise in her throat. She closed her eyes. *God, I am so nervous. The worst thing that could happen would be that this was all a big misunderstanding, and they didn't know my parents.* The thought sent a renewed wave of nausea through her. *Dear Jesus, I pray they knew my family.*

Knowing that sitting in the car and stewing about it wouldn't get her in the hotel any faster, she opened the car door and slipped out. After attempting to flatten the wrinkles in her capris, she picked up her purse and hefted the strap onto her shoulder.

Please, Lord, let them like me.

❧

Josif had never before witnessed such an instantaneous bonding between his mother and another person. Mirela soaked in every word his mother said. Mama grabbed both of Mirela's cheeks in her hands. "It is like looking at my dear friend Jovana again."

Papa raised his hand in the air. "Ah, but she has her father's dimple in her cheek."

Mama nodded. "That she does."

"There you are. I brought you some cake."

Josif turned to find Sabrina holding a plate out to him. He took it and nodded toward two seats. "Thank you."

They sat down, and Josif took a bite of the cake. It was his mother's homemade red velvet and cream cheese. He closed his eyes to savor each morsel. Scrumptious.

"Your mother and Mirela seem to be hitting it off." Sabrina pointed toward them.

He noticed Sofija had joined Mirela and his mother. Mirela held the journal they had written. She seemed absorbed in every word, as if it were a child's first Christmas. Her excitement made her more beautiful, and he found himself yearning to learn more about her and the family his parents used to know. "Yes, they are."

"Your mother's never taken that much interest in me."

Josif looked at his girlfriend. Her eyes were downcast, her bottom lip puckered into a pout. He tried to put himself in Sabrina's position. His mother hadn't taken a real interest in Sabrina, but the behavior was mutual. Sabrina never wanted to visit with his family members, never offered to go to dinner with them or join them at one of his nephews' ballgames. As a couple, they'd even turned down several offerings.

He'd never realized Sabrina was so selfish. Mirela was his mother's dead friend's daughter from Serbia. The chances of seeing her again had been less than slim. Only God could have brought them together. And He had done just that, and all his girlfriend could say was that his mother didn't pay enough attention to her.

The room was suddenly stifling. He loosened the top button on his polo shirt and stood. "Excuse me, Sabrina. I'll be right back."

After making his way out of the room, he went into the restroom. He turned on the cold water and splashed some on his face. Pulling several paper towels out of the dispenser, he stared at his reflection then wiped off the water. He'd dated Sabrina for three years, and in less than one week, he'd begun to see a side of her that he didn't understand. Couldn't stomach.

God, have I been so wrapped up in work that I've been blind to the people around me? He could count on one hand the times he'd passed a ball with his nephews, and the oldest was already twelve. He wasn't even sure what grade his nine-year-old nephew was in. He'd attended church with his family every Sunday, but that was all. He'd been too busy to help with any ministries or enjoy any fellowship. Sabrina's church life mimicked his. She sat beside him in the pew every week, but she didn't participate in anything else.

He remembered his preacher's words one Sunday morning: "If you were on trial for being a Christian, would there be enough evidence to convict you?"

A chill swept down Josif's spine. He knew the answer.

Brushing the thought away, he walked back to the conference room. He wouldn't let Sabrina get to him. Not today. This day belonged to his mother and Mirela.

Out of the corner of his eye, he spied Sabrina talking with his brother-in-law. Her animated motions and expressions proved she was frustrated about something. Sofija's saint of a husband, Matt, stood still, arms crossed in front of his chest, and nodded at whatever she said.

Determined to stay out of the way, Josif pulled up a chair beside his mother. She pointed to the journal. "When your mother carried you, she wanted my soda bread." Mama placed her hand on her forehead. "Soda bread. Soda bread. Soda bread. Praise God, soda bread is cheap. She could never get her fill of it."

Mirela laughed. "I believe I'd like to try your soda bread."

Mama tapped her leg. "Then you shall. We will have it the next time you come to visit."

Josif winced. He didn't like soda bread at all. He'd rather have a warm buttermilk biscuit with a slathering a homemade apple butter. Or a thick slice of corn bread covered with butter.

Mirela looked at her watch and sighed. "It is getting late. My mother will be worried, and church is tomorrow. I teach Sunday school."

"What age do you teach?" asked Sofija.

Mirela grinned. "Babies."

Mama looked at Josif and winked. She patted his leg and clucked her tongue. "Did you hear that, Josif? Just like her mother, Jovana. Always with the babies."

Warmth trailed up his neck and jaw. He knew what she implied, but going by the confused expression on Mirela's face, *she* had no idea. Which was good. She didn't need to hear about Mama's matchmaking.

Mirela grabbed his mother's hand. "We have to plan to see each other again."

"Can you come to dinner this week? I will fix all Serbian foods."

Josif's stomach fell. He hated his native cuisine. Too many fast food hamburgers and greasy pizzas had worked their way into clotting his arteries and satisfying his taste buds. On any given day and for any meal, he'd take American food and its version of different food cultures over the food of his youth.

Mirela beamed. "That would be wonderful. What about Tuesday?"

"Tuesday is perfect." His mother cupped Mirela's face in her hand. "I cannot wait to see you again."

six

Mirela opened the front door and found her mother sitting in the rocking chair, holding a sleeping Benny in her arms. She furrowed her brows. "Mom, what's going on?"

Sarah lifted a finger to her puckered lips then patted Benny's bottom. "I've just gotten him to sleep." The baby shifted and lifted his head off her shoulder then pressed his cheek against her mother once again.

"Has something happened to Emily or Bella?"

Her mother shook her head and whispered, "His mother and sister are fine. They've just come down with some kind of stomach bug." Benny's eyelids fluttered and he sucked his bottom lip. "Let me lay him down then we'll talk."

Mirela tossed her purse on the chair then reached for the baby. "I'll do it. I know what position he prefers."

Sarah nodded, and Mirela gently lifted him off her mother's shoulder and nestled him against her. She started down the hall then paused. "Mom, where am I taking him?"

She chuckled. "I have his portable playpen set up in your room." She winked. "I figured he'd be happiest if he woke up to someone he knew."

Mirela nodded. Employed as a nurse in the neonatal unit, her mother could easily care for the baby, but she was right, Benny would feel more comfortable with Mirela. He felt so warm and contented against her. She loved the way his chubby fingers splayed across her neck. The sound of his deep breathing made her lift him and press a slight kiss on

47

his pink cheek. He smelled of laundry detergent and baby lotion.

As she laid him in the playpen, she wished for her own baby. She was old enough. It was time. But God hadn't brought a husband into her life. Josif's face when he'd welcomed her into the hotel flashed through her mind. She needed to stop thinking of him. He had a girlfriend. *An unbelievably gorgeous girlfriend.*

Benny whimpered, and she placed his pacifier in his mouth then patted his bottom. He settled down and fell back to dreamland with a deep sigh. Mirela sneaked out of the room and gently shut the door behind her.

Her mother still sat in the rocking chair with her head pressed against the back and her eyes closed. Mama Sesely had said her birthmother had had a way with babies. Mirela's adopted mother did as well. And babies always had a soothing effect on Mirela. When Mirela had left for Gatlinburg, her mom refused to say good-bye, but only a moment ago she agreed to talk.

Mirela went into the kitchen and grabbed a water bottle out of the refrigerator. She made her way back into the living room, slipped off her sandals, then sat in the love seat, folding her legs under her. Her mother opened her eyes and smiled at Mirela. "I'm glad your friend called. Emily seemed hesitant to bring Benny without you here, but I've enjoyed my time with him. What a precious baby."

"She brought him for a stomach bug?" Mirela had taken Benny and his older sister Bella to church with her on several occasions, but she'd never kept Benny overnight.

A piteous expression wrapped her mother's face. "His mama was sick. She called for you. Before I could tell her you weren't here, she had to excuse herself to throw up. I told her to bring him on over, and she threw up here before she could leave. I think his sister was just as bad." Her mother shook her head as she tightened the belt of her robe. "I think I'll call and check on them in the morning before church."

Mirela picked up her purse to search for her cell phone. "Maybe I should check on them now."

Sarah raised her hand to stop her. "Let her rest while she can. She seems to carry quite a burden. Said she doesn't have any family around here."

"Her parents live in North Carolina. From what I understand she has a lot of siblings, but they're all young and still living at home."

Nodding, her mom stood. "I think I'd like some coffee. Would you like a cup? It's already brewed."

Mirela shook her head and lifted up her water bottle. "I'm fine. Where's Ivy?"

"She's at the church for game night."

Her mom shuffled toward the kitchen. Mirela could tell her arthritis was acting up. She hoped watching Benny hadn't been too much for her. "Have you taken your medicine, Mom?"

Her mother grimaced as she shuffled back into the living room with a cup of coffee in one hand and a pill in the other. "Getting ready to take it right now."

She lowered herself back down into the rocking chair and swallowed the pill with a swig of java. She let out a long breath and rocked lightly with her foot. "It's a nice evening, isn't it?"

Irritation rose in Mirela's chest. Her mother refused to say good-bye to her when she left that afternoon, and now she was making small talk about the weather. It grated on Mirela that her mom didn't act the slightest bit interested in the

Sesely family or what Mirela had learned about her past. Her mother hadn't even asked if she'd discovered the Seselys were who she'd thought they were.

How could the woman have raised her for the past nineteen years and not understand Mirela's need to know something about her biological family? Wouldn't Sarah want Ivy to learn about her if they had been separated by tragedy? Mirela stared at the woman who'd cared for her for most of her life, rocking as if nothing in the world had changed.

Mirela believed she and her mother were close. She'd cried on her shoulder when she lost the fourth-grade spelling bee. She'd called her mother to come get her at the middle school party that turned into a mean girl session. She'd eagerly shared when her sophomore boyfriend surreptitiously pecked her with a kiss before math class. Her mother and sister were the two people in the world Mirela could be herself with. She didn't blush when they spoke to her, nor stutter when they argued with her.

And this should be something that she could share with her mom.

"Would you like to know how my trip to Gatlinburg went?"

"Was the traffic heavy?"

Mirela pursed her lips. "Yes. As a matter of fact, it was."

"Hmm." Her mother continued to rock, but Mirela noted she seemed to move a bit faster.

"Would you like to know anything else?"

"Did you have trouble finding your destination?"

Mirela swallowed. "No, actually, I didn't." She cleared her throat. "Anything else?"

Her mother pressed her lips together as she looked at the ceiling, then at the window, then at Mirela. "No. There isn't anything else I'd like to ask."

Mirela uncurled her legs and leaned forward, pressing her elbows on her knees. "You wouldn't like to know about the Sesely family, and if they did know my birth parents, or if they knew anything about my history?"

Her mother's gaze bored into hers. Mirela sat back in the chair, surprised at the anger she saw glaring back at her. "No, Mirela. I do not want to know anything about any of that."

Waves of hurt washed over the irritation, and Mirela felt tears pool in her eyes. "But—"

Her mother lifted her index finger in the air as she stood. "Not one word."

A knife sliced through her as Mirela watched her mother hobble back into the kitchen. She jumped at the smash of the coffee cup landing in the sink then her mother's bedroom door shutting. Hard.

Rejection and confusion laced through Mirela. She didn't understand her mother's anger. It boggled her mind and tore at her heart.

৯

Josif reached for a towel. He grabbed the shut-off valve to stop the spewing of water from one of the hotel's kitchen sinks. The knob wouldn't budge. He yelled at the kitchen help. "Turn off the water! Someone get me a wrench!"

While one employee ran outside to turn off the water, another rummaged through a closet until he found a wrench. Josif yanked it from the young man's grasp, tightened it on the valve, and turned it until the water slowed to a trickle. Within moments, the water had been turned off and the trickle stopped as well.

Josif released the wrench and stood. He shook the water from his hair then wiped his face with his hand and flicked off the excess water. He looked up at the clock. Mirela's church started in an hour. He couldn't possibly take care of this mess and get his parents there on time.

He peered up at the ceiling. "Thank you, Lord."

The night before, Josif had spent two full hours trying to convince his mother that they shouldn't visit Mirela at her church the very day after they'd met her. His mother was excited to have a piece of her best friend back, but he didn't want her to overwhelm their new friend either. Mirela had seemed much more at ease last night than the day he'd met her. *I probably did surprise her on our first meeting.*

Still, her ease the evening before did not constitute his entire family loading up in a van and meeting her unexpectedly for church. She'd agreed to return for dinner on Tuesday. His mother needed to wait until then to see her again. *Although I wouldn't mind seeing her again either.*

"Josif, what has happened?" His mother ran into the kitchen, her hands cupping both sides of her face.

He shrugged. "Pipe burst? I don't know. I'll call a plumber." He reached for his phone in his back pocket. It was soaked like the rest of him. "Oh no." He snatched a towel off a shelf and patted his treasured device. He pulled off the back and snapped out the battery. Maybe if he put it in a tub of rice it would dry out. The last thing he needed to do was purchase another phone.

Taking a step in the pooled water, he splashed some on his mother's leg. He looked at her. Her expression had fallen into the despair of someone who'd just lost a loved one. He turned and wrapped a wet arm around her shoulder. "I'm sorry, Mama."

Instead of pushing away from his soggy frame, she wrapped her arms around him. "I miss her so much already."

Regret for his thoughts swelled within him. He couldn't possibly understand all that his Serbian mama and papa had lost when they'd left the Croatian land of Krajina. He'd seen them look at pictures, witnessed the sadness that covered their faces as they watched televised newscasts of their fellow Serbians being forced to leave the only homes they'd known in Croatia because of ethnic cleansing. His parents had spent their lives scraping for a way to bring their family to a land of freedom. They had achieved their goal but lost a lot in the process. Mirela was more than just the daughter of an old friend. She was a connection to the bulk of his mother's life. He kissed the top of her head. "We will get to see her again on Tuesday."

Mama sniffed and nodded. "Yes. You are right." She started toward the door. "I will send Papa to come help as soon as he gets out of the shower."

"No, Mama. I will take care of it. You and Papa go to our church." His father hated to drive. Made him nervous. But he was willing to make the short drive to their church if the need arose.

She didn't look back, just nodded as she left the kitchen.

Josif turned to the hotel staff. "Go ahead and start cleaning up the water." He looked at his watch. "I'll see if I can find a plumber."

He bit back a growl as his new shoes splashed through the puddle on the floor. The plumber he usually used attended their church. Josif hated the idea of calling the man only an hour before services started, but he knew his friend would need the work.

Sabrina showed up at the door, holding a tray of coffees and a bag of muffins. "I heard about the pipe." She set the tray on one of the metal cabinets. "I brought some breakfast for everyone while you clean it up."

Josif smiled. With her hair pulled back in a loose ponytail, she didn't look as stiff as she had the last few times they'd been together. Here was the Sabrina he knew and cared about. "That was very kind of you."

"What can I do to help?"

He shook his head. "Not a thing. You've done enough already. I'll get ahold of a plumber. You can go on to church."

She crinkled her nose and frowned. "Nonsense. Church will still be there next week. I'll stay right here and help."

Josif headed toward his office with Sabrina beside him. *It was really nice that she brought breakfast to the workers.* He repeated the thought several times in his mind, but he couldn't stifle the concern he felt at her nonchalant attitude about their time of worship.

seven

Mirela could barely keep her eyes open. She'd kept Benny two nights in a row, and he'd slept only a few hours each night. He'd thrown up several times Saturday night and Sunday morning. Thankfully, the bug seemed to pass, but sickness had still clung to Emily Sunday night, and Mirela had offered to keep him again. And he didn't sleep again.

She pushed a strand of hair from her eyes. *At least he wasn't sick all night. Just awake.* She peered at the baby who slept like a cherub in the bouncy seat while Zach and Callie kicked and cooed at her from their seats. She longed to curl up beside Benny and rest her eyes as well.

But she couldn't. She had a job to do. She tapped her cheek with her hand. No snoozing on the clock. She pried her eyelids open with her fingers and looked at the sleeping child. "I don't know how your mommy does it."

Ivy had already promised that if Emily was still sick, she would take care of Benny that evening so Mirela could take a nap. She peered up at the lamb-shaped clock. It was only 10:30, and she had seven hours to go.

Cheryl opened the top Dutch door. "Mirela, would you mind watching the two-year-olds for a minute?"

Not really in the mood to work two jobs, Mirela snapped, "Just for a minute."

Cheryl cocked her head and scrunched her face as if she was about to say something. Normally Mirela would apologize for asking the woman not to take too long. Today she was simply too tired to deal with Cheryl trying to get out of doing her job. Cheryl huffed and opened the bottom Dutch door before walking out with her cell phone in her right hand.

Mirela knew she'd call her boyfriend and argue with him for half an hour before returning to take care of the kids. Madi toddled into the room and handed Mirela a plastic drumstick. "Eat, Miss Mela."

She took the drumstick from the girl's hand and pretended to gobble it up. She shouldn't get so frustrated with Cheryl. The woman wasn't a Christian. She needed Jesus, and if watching the children a little bit each day gave Mirela the opportunity to show Cheryl who Jesus was and what He was about, then she'd watch those kiddos with a cheerful heart.

"Doormats aren't examples of Jesus." Ivy's words at one of the youth meetings flashed through Mirela's mind. Her sister had been sharing with the teen girls how they needed to live life proud of their faith and purity, not in piety or pompousness, but in humility and truth. She'd also told them not to be doormats. The comment stuck to Mirela like cradle cap to a newborn's scalp. Too often she allowed people to walk on her.

At home she inwardly fumed and stewed over her mom's unwillingness to speak of the Sesely family, but she didn't say anything. At work she grew weary and sometimes wasn't able to complete her job as she would like because Cheryl took too many long breaks, but she continued to allow her to do it.

I'm a doormat, God.

Her spirit stirred within her, reminding her of sparrows who could not fall to the ground without God's knowledge, and how she was worth more than many birds. And how God clothed the lilies of the valley with more splendor than

Solomon, despite all his riches. God cared for her.

I know what Your Word says, Lord. I know I am special, but does that mean I should stand up to Cheryl? Shouldn't I turn the other cheek? I would rather just do the work myself than have to confront and perhaps upset others.

She thought of Jesus' anger at the people selling and buying in the temple courts. He'd overturned tables and reprimanded them for their actions. His had been a righteous anger at the disrespect shown to God's holy place.

"Don't you see, you are My holy temple as well."

She blinked at the thought. God dwelled within her as her Redeemer and Lord, and she knew His word said not to do anything to harm her body—but to confront someone over unnecessarily long breaks? It seemed petty and unnecessary.

But if she couldn't do her own job well, if the children weren't cared for in the way their parents expected because she was too busy changing diapers to read books or had to rush through bottle feedings to play house. . . . Maybe she did need to speak with Cheryl.

She mentally shook off her thoughts as one of the two-year-olds handed her a book to read. She couldn't think about this now. She was tired. She needed to be alone with God and her Bible to sift through these thoughts. Maybe Ivy would have some insight. She opened the cardboard book to the first page. For now, she needed to work.

❧

Tuesday was not going as expected. Having received a text message from Sofija, Josif sneaked into his mother's darkened bedroom. She held a pillow over her head. She must have sensed his presence because she said, "The food is ready. Please take it. The smell is making me sick."

Migraines plagued his mother about once a month. He

could hear the frustration and sadness in her voice. "I'm sorry, Mama."

She didn't respond, and he knew she must be in a great deal of pain. He headed to the kitchen where he grabbed the pot of paprikash, a Serbian goulash, as well as the soda bread she'd made. It was a meal he never enjoyed, almost always avoided, and now he and Mirela would dine on it—alone.

He hefted the pot and bread to the same conference room they'd used to meet her the first time. The whole family was supposed to enjoy dinner with Mirela. But Sofija's oldest son had fallen during recess, and they were still at the hospital getting stitches in his hand. His mother was stuck in bed with a migraine, and his father refused to leave their apartment. Sabrina had gone to dinner with some of her sorority friends. That left just him and Mirela.

He took down two plates from the cabinet in the room then grabbed two silverware settings. He didn't know what Mirela would think when she learned she'd have to eat dinner with him alone. Because his mother's migraine had come up suddenly, he wondered if she'd just been trying to ignore the signs so she wouldn't miss seeing Mirela.

He rubbed his hands together. There was nothing he could do about it now. It was too late to call and cancel.

Mirela walked into the conference room. Her hair was clipped up on the sides, but the bulk of it flowed down her back. She wore a pale-yellow sundress that stopped at her knees. The color suited her sun-kissed skin. She gripped the strap of her bag as she glanced around the room. "Am I early?"

Josif shook his head. "I'm afraid it's just you and me tonight."

"Oh." She looked down at the floor then shifted her

weight from one foot to the other.

He explained everything, and she allowed him a hesitant smile, but he could tell she was still uncomfortable. He motioned toward an empty chair. "Mama made Serbian goulash and soda bread, just as she said. She'll be crushed if we don't eat it."

Mirela placed her hand on her chest. "Of course, we'll eat it." She sat in the chair, unfolded the napkin, and placed it in her lap. He pulled out another chair and sat across from her. He reached for the ladle to hand to her when he noticed she held both hands out to him across the table.

Heat shot through him as he realized she wanted to say grace. His family blessed their meals when eating together, so it wasn't a foreign idea to him. But he couldn't recall the last time he and Sabrina had prayed over a meal. And never at her suggestion.

He placed his hands in Mirela's. Guilt washed over him. Her hands felt nice in his. Soft and warm. He didn't want to let them go. But he had a girlfriend, and he shouldn't be thinking such things. Holding hands with a woman to say grace meant nothing. Mirela would probably laugh aloud if she could read his thoughts.

He gazed at Mirela. She obviously didn't feel the connection he felt. She merely whispered, "Do you mind saying grace?"

"Of course not." He tried to break his gaze from hers, but she'd worn some kind of pink eye color on her lids, making the brown in her eyes dance in the light. He wanted to know her thoughts, what made her so intriguing, and why she was able to draw him in so quickly. He prided himself on being a staunch businessman, fair and honest, but able to put emotions to the side. But Mirela made his mind whirl with ponderings he'd never considered.

Forcing his eyes closed, he bowed his head. "Lord, bless this food. Thank You that we found Mirela." She squeezed his hands, and it felt as if every ounce of blood in his body rushed to his toes. "May we enjoy our time tonight. Amen."

He lifted his gaze up to hers again. She pulled her hand away then shook her finger at him. "You didn't pray for your mother or your nephew."

He ducked his head. This was exactly what he'd meant—Mirela's presence threw him off kilter, made him forget things he should remember. He squinted his eyes shut and reached for her hands again and squeezed. "And, Lord, heal Mama and Ross." He opened his eyes and released her hands. "There. Now I remembered."

Mirela laughed. It was a soft sound, yet somehow it filled the room. "I suppose it will have to do." She pointed to her chest. "Good thing God knows the heart."

Josif uncovered the pot. The smell of the paprikash turned his stomach. He had never been a fan of lamb. He disliked it even more now that he had his own place with his preferred foods in the refrigerator. He grabbed the ladle, scooped a portion of the goulash onto her plate, then onto his. Mirela picked up the soda bread and pulled off a chunk, and he did the same.

Peering down at the meal he'd have to force himself to eat, Josif took a deep breath and shoveled a bit of paprikash into his mouth. He raised his eyebrows and smiled at Mirela as he watched her chew on a piece of the bread. Swallowing hard, he noticed she chewed a few moments longer and then took a sip of water. She seemed hesitant to take a bite of the Serbian goulash. He shoveled in another bite as she brought her fork to her mouth. She shoved the food in and swallowed without chewing. Josif watched as she took another quick drink of water.

He put down his fork and wiped his mouth. "So what do you think?"

She cleared her throat. "It's different. I'm used to—"

He leaned closer to her. "I hate it."

Her gaze searched his then a smile spread across her lips. "It's not that. . ."

He waved his hands in front of her. "Really. You don't have to explain. I would much rather have a greasy hamburger or some General Tso's chicken."

"Mmm, I love sweet and sour chicken."

An idea popped into his head, and he placed the napkin on the table. "Let's clean this up, and I'll take you to one of my favorite Chinese restaurants. It's a small establishment, so many of the tourists miss it, but it has the best noodles in town."

Mirela giggled. He loved the sound of her voice. It soothed him, made him forget about all the worries of the day.

&

Mirela and Josif walked through the front doors of the Chinese restaurant. The dining area was very small, seating only fifty or fewer people. The decor was fun, if not a bit tacky. Paper fans and lanterns hung from the ceiling, and Chinese artwork that appeared to be copied on colored paper hung on the walls. Beside the register sat a huge fish tank sporting several blue and orange fishes. An Asian woman greeted them and guided them to a booth toward the kitchen area.

Josif slid in the seat across from Mirela. "Although I love the food here, I rarely get to come."

"Why?"

"I work a lot." He opened his hands. "And no one likes Chinese but me."

She intertwined her fingers and placed her hands on the table. "Then I'm glad we could come."

Josif shifted in his seat then unbuttoned the top of his polo shirt. She noticed he did that a lot. He probably hated wearing a button-down shirt and tie during the hotel's office hours. "So how was work?"

Mirela shared about keeping Benny for the weekend. "I adore the little munchkin, but he sure didn't like sleeping in a different place."

The waitress appeared then took their orders. Mirela looked back at Josif and realized he was studying her.

He picked at the corner of the napkin. "It was very nice of you to help your friend."

She furrowed her eyebrows. "Of course, I'd help her. You'd help your family or friends."

A flash of confusion zipped across his face as if her words hit him in the chest unprepared. He masked the expression quickly. "But you like caring for children?"

"I do. It's one of the reasons the shoebox ministry is so dear to my heart. I love to see the excitement in the faces of small children, to watch the wonderment in their eyes when they learn a new thing."

She told him about Madi and how she'd learned to count to twenty, which Mirela found to be an amazing feat for a just-turned-two-year-old. "But then Madi has always been more vocal than most children."

Her face heated when the waitress showed up with their meals. Mirela had been talking nonstop since they'd sat down. And about babies and toddlers. He must be bored out of his mind. "I'm sorry, Josif. I haven't let you get a word in.

Tell me about the hotel."

Josif smiled at her, a smile that once again made her toes curl in her sandals. "Your passion for the children is obvious."

"It's God given, that's for sure."

"Your faith is obvious as well."

Mirela crinkled the napkin in her hand. "That's the best compliment you could possibly give me."

Silence fell between them as they took bites of their food. Josif was right. The noodles were amazing. She started to tell him so, but something held her back. He seemed to focus intently on his food. Something she'd said had apparently stirred something in him, but she couldn't tell what. *God, I hope I didn't offend him or say something I shouldn't have.*

Although shy by nature, she'd also been known to say things she should have kept locked behind her lips. It was the weirdest combination. Talk little, but when you talk, insert foot into mouth. She inwardly chuckled. *God, You made me this way.*

"How is it?"

Josif's question brought her thoughts back to the dinner. "Delicious."

"Good." He pulled his phone from his back pocket, presumably checking the time or perhaps his messages. "I don't mean to rush you, but I'll have to be getting back soon."

His formal tone straightened her in the seat. She'd definitely said something that offended him. She pondered the conversation in her mind as she shoveled the food that should have been savored into her mouth. For the life of her, she couldn't figure out what she'd said.

eight

Mirela tried to keep the queasiness in her stomach at bay as she and Ivy hiked their favorite trek up the mountain. Surely she would feel better if she could just be sick and get it over with. But she couldn't, and she knew it wouldn't help anyway. Her sickness wasn't from illness. It was her attraction to a man who had a girlfriend.

She grabbed her stomach as she followed Ivy on what felt like a never-ending incline. She should be enjoying God's nature. The land would only be rich and green a few weeks longer. Not that she didn't love the deep oranges, reds, salmons, and yellows of the fall. She basked in the beauty of the autumn colors, but she didn't want to pass up the grandeur of today because she was stewing on a man she couldn't have.

"Moving a little slow today, aren't you?"

Mirela stopped and looked up at her sister. She intertwined her fingers and placed her hands above her head. "I know."

Concern traced Ivy's features. "Are you sick?"

"I don't know."

Ivy studied her for a moment, and Mirela knew her sister could see it was more than just a physical ailment bothering her. But Mirela didn't want to talk about it. Talking wouldn't do any good.

Besides it wasn't just Josif. It was work and Cheryl and knowing when to stand up to her and when to turn the other cheek. It was Emily and her kids. Lately, Emily had been picking up Benny even later than usual, and she'd been acting funny. Mirela couldn't quite put her finger on it. And it was Josif, and the fact that she noticed all his quirks and could hear his voice at any given moment of her day.

She should simply be thankful for the opportunity to get to know Josif and his family. Having them find her was a wish she hadn't even known to ask for. It was just selfishness, plain and simple, that she couldn't stop thinking about him. She'd never before behaved this way over a man.

She bit the inside of her lip. That wasn't completely true. In seventh grade, she'd had such a miserable crush on Johnny Combs that she didn't sleep for days and could barely eat. She'd even gotten sick and had to run to the bathroom and vomit when he'd spoken to her at lunch. She inwardly chuckled. *I guess I have behaved this way over a boy before.*

Straightening her shoulders, she took quick, even steps to keep pace with her sister. She'd gotten over Johnny Combs, and she'd get over Josif Sesely.

After a few more minutes of hiking, they reached their destination. Mirela flopped onto the bench that overlooked the valley and several rolling hills. She and God had spent many a day on this very bench; sometimes she worshipped Him in prayer or song, and sometimes He spoke to her heart through the sounds of His creation. She closed her eyes. Today would be a day of listening. She didn't have the strength, inside or out, for anything else. She needed God to wrap His arms around her and hold her for a while.

"You want to talk about it?"

Mirela opened her eyes and saw Ivy studying her. Mirela shook her head. "Not yet."

Ivy nodded. "I understand." She pointed to her backpack.

"I brought my novel with me. I'm going to head up a little farther and read awhile."

Mirela closed her eyes again. "Sounds good."

She heard her sister's tennis shoes crunch as Ivy journeyed a few more yards away. She pictured the verse in Matthew where Jesus told the weary to come to Him so He could give them rest. *I need You, God. I need Your peace and Your truth.*

In her mind, she saw arms open wide, beckoning her to come and let Him hold her a little while. She wouldn't argue with Him. She needed her Abba's refreshing embrace.

❧

For too many reasons, it had been the longest five days of his life. He pulled at the necktie Mama insisted he wear to church. Normally he'd simply wear a polo shirt. But even they felt as if they were choking him.

He peered around the unfamiliar sanctuary. Mirela's church was much smaller than theirs. Only two sets of pews extended out from the center pulpit. A piano sat on the left side of the stage and an organ on the right. The people had been friendly in welcoming him and his family to their church, but he still wondered what Mirela would think of them showing up without telling her.

Sabrina held tight to his hand and pressed herself against his arm. Her perfume wafted into his nostrils. He'd always liked the fragrance, but today his stomach turned. Maybe he was just nervous.

And he hadn't slept much. Mirela's comment about helping his friends and family when they needed him had haunted him. The time when his brother-in-law and sister and the kids had a flat tire with no spare kept flooding his mind. He and Sabrina had been on a date, already in the movie theater with soft drinks and popcorn.

Matt called him for help. Sabrina had thrown a fit until Josif finally persuaded his father, who hated driving, to pick up his sister and family. He'd felt like such a jerk, but he still sat there and watched some dumb movie instead of helping them. *I don't even remember what we watched.*

The selfishness in that one action ate at him, and then brought on an onslaught of other selfish choices he'd made the last few years. Each time Sabrina had been part of why he wasn't there for his family. He wouldn't blame her for his actions. She didn't force him to do anything, but when he was around her he wasn't happy with the person he'd become.

He'd prayed more the last five days than he had in three years. Hours of prayer and Bible study. He'd hungered for God's Word, even reading little snippets between hotel duties. He didn't want to be the man he saw in the mirror. He'd been doing it all wrong. It should be God first, family second, and then his job.

"This place is so. . .small."

Sabrina's snide tone grated his nerves. He'd gone from mentally preparing himself to potentially propose marriage to being unable to stay in the same room with her for very long. He felt like a traitor to her. Like a turncoat. His thoughts and feelings had shifted so fast. But he needed to place God at the center of his life, and Sabrina didn't encourage that. He wasn't even sure if she was truly a Christian.

Which made him feel even worse. He needed to be praying for her, to encourage her in faith. Instead he dreaded being around her.

"Mama Sesely!"

Mirela's excited voice sounded from two rows behind them. The family turned, and Mirela wrapped his mother in a huge hug. "I'm so glad you're here."

Mirela looked a bit paler, maybe a pound or two thinner. Mama had called Mirela to apologize for not being able to see her on paprikash night. Mirela relayed she'd gotten sick, having caught Benny's stomach bug on Wednesday. Mama had been devastated. She'd hoped Mirela would return to Gatlinburg to see them by the weekend. When she couldn't, Mama insisted they visit her church.

Mirela hugged Papa then turned toward Josif and Sabrina. "Sabrina, that dress is so pretty."

Sabrina tightened her grip on his hand. "Thank you."

Mirela waved over a young blond woman in a bright pink dress. The woman practically ran to them then covered her mouth with her hands and bounced in front of them. "Is this them?"

Mirela nodded. "Mama and Papa Sesely, Josif and Sabrina, this is my sister, Ivy." After introducing her sister, Mirela motioned to an older version of Ivy, standing in the foyer. The woman scowled then returned to her conversation with another lady.

Ivy grabbed Mama's hand and shook it. "It's so good to meet you. Mirela has been so excited."

Mama touched Mirela's cheek. "Seeing her is God's gift to me. How I loved her mother."

The older woman who looked like Ivy approached them with her hand extended. They shook hands. "I'm Sarah Adams, Mirela's mother. It's nice to meet you."

Mama gushed over the woman, telling her what a good job she'd done with Jovana's daughter. Though his mother didn't seem to notice, Josif could tell the woman was uncomfortable with the meeting. After several minutes, she nodded. "Well, it's almost time to start." She pointed toward the other side of the church. "Girls, we should be seated."

"I believe I'll sit with them today, Mom." Mirela's words slipped through gritted teeth. "Why don't you join me?"

She shook her head. "My things are already in my seat." She looked at Mama. "It was nice to meet you. Come on, Ivy."

Ivy wrinkled her nose and shrugged. She looked from his mother to his father to him and Sabrina. "It really was a treat to meet you all."

The family slid into the pew, with Mirela sitting between his mother and Sabrina. He could tell Mirela had tensed up since her mother introduced herself. He wondered why the woman would be so upset with them showing up at the church. She'd been a missionary to his people. Surely she would be thrilled for Mirela to meet some of the people from her past. Wouldn't she?

Mirela tried to focus on the service, but she simply fumed. Although she was thrilled Mama and Papa Sesely had shown up for church, she was upset that her mother hadn't been even remotely kind to them. Her and her mom's relationship had been stilted all week. Mom simply refused to allow the Sesely name to be mentioned in the house, and Mirela had no idea why.

Ivy had been at a loss as well. Several times her sister had tried to talk with Mom at dinner or before work or while they did the dishes. Mom would have no part of it. She would either get angry or walk away. She'd taken many walks the last week. All by herself. It was something their mother did when she was battling some kind of inner turmoil.

God, the turmoil needs to stop. Her behavior isn't Christlike.

"You just don't see my side of things!" Cheryl's furious words to her boyfriend on Friday replayed in Mirela's mind. She frowned. What did that have to do with her mother?

She sneaked a peek at her mom and Ivy. She knew her

sister. Ivy studied their pastor's words, jotting down notes as she did every week. Her mother sat rigid, almost cold, beside her. Mirela had never seen her mother like this. Something was going on.

God, help me see Mom's point of view. I simply don't understand.

She thought of how good her mother was to the people she knew, friends and even strangers. Her family had made more meals than she could count for families who were struggling with sickness. They'd collected food and clothes for the needy, visited nursing homes and food pantries. Their basement was practically filled to capacity with items for Christmas shoeboxes. Her mother had a good heart. She was a godly woman. So what was causing her to be so upset about Mirela getting to know the Sesely family? Until that was resolved, Mirela needed to exhibit patience and respect her mother.

The service ended, and to Mirela's surprise Mom walked up to them. "We'd love it if your family would join us for lunch. Nothing fancy. We'll just grill hamburgers and have chips.

"That sounds wonderful. Thank you for your hospitality," said Mama Sesely.

Mirela looked at her sister and raised her eyebrows. Ivy shrugged, and the two of them smiled at each other. Mirela followed the family to their van. She could tell Sabrina didn't want to join her family for lunch, but she held her tongue and Mirela was glad. Maybe if Mom spent time with them, she'd see how terrific they were.

Once at her house, Mirela guided the family inside. Mama Sesely joined Mom and Ivy in the kitchen while Josif, Sabrina, and Papa Sesely sat in the living room. She handed Josif the remote and he turned on a preseason NFL game. Sabrina looked as if she would pummel him the moment she had the chance.

Mirela walked through the kitchen. "I'll start the grill, Mom."

Her mother nodded, and she and Mama Sesely went back to pulling different foods from the refrigerator and cabinets.

Mirela stepped onto the deck. She turned on the propane and then pushed the grill's starter button. She stared at the rolling hills just beyond her backyard. So much had changed in a week's time. She didn't know everything about her past life, but she knew more than she'd ever dreamed possible. For the millionth time, she wondered about her older sister and her cousins. She longed to see them again, to witness to them. Maybe during this year's shoebox trip, she would have the opportunity. She prayed she might.

Ivy stepped through the back door with a plateful of uncooked hamburgers and hotdogs. "Where's the beef?"

Mirela laughed at their constant joke about the 1980s fast-food commercial. They'd found it one day when they were searching YouTube for a commercial one of their friends told them about. They'd giggled over the advertisement ever since. "Looks like you've got the beef."

"Indeed, I do." Ivy set the plate beside the grill, and Mirela opened the lid. Ivy nodded back toward the house. "That fellow in there is pretty beefy, too."

Mirela gasped and bumped Ivy's hip. "Ivy, he has a girlfriend."

She lifted her hands in surrender. "The guy can still be cute, can't he?"

"Well, yes, but—"

"But nothing. He's a hottie." Ivy sneaked a peek over her shoulder. "And he keeps looking at you."

Mirela glanced through the patio door. She'd thought of Josif Sesely more times this week than she cared to admit. She hated that she already knew he drank one soda then water with his meals, that he scratched his jaw when he was thinking, that he hated to wear things tight around his neck. She shouldn't notice things like that about a man who had a girlfriend, especially a drop-dead gorgeous one. She'd loathed it when girls in school stole each other's boyfriends. She would never be that kind of girl.

She peered at her sister. "I am not interested in someone else's boyfriend."

Now she wished she could convince herself.

nine

Josif hadn't seen Mirela for two weeks. He hadn't seen much of Sabrina either. She had gone on a trip to Florida with her college sorority friends and had just returned yesterday. She planned for them to have dinner that evening, but he wasn't looking forward to it. That bothered him. He should want to spend time with his girlfriend.

But he'd been busy. Football season had started, and he'd watched his beloved Colts, as well as caught Tennessee's first home game. He'd also had time to hash some more things out with God.

His hands moved across Matthew 6:21, the verse he'd paraphrased and placed inside the middle drawer of his desk: *Where your treasure is, there your heart is.* He'd written beneath it: *Where is my treasure?* The question was to serve as a daily reminder to ask and then allow God to guide the answer.

Besides spending more time with his family, he also discovered the need to be more complimentary of his staff. With peppermints weighing down his pockets, he made his way toward the pool area. He waved to guests, but when he saw one of his employees working hard, he'd stop, shake the person's hand, and give him or her a peppermint. The immediate positive response amazed him. Such a small token of appreciation and acknowledgement meant so much.

It shouldn't have surprised him. He'd always enjoyed a pat on the back from his father for doing a good job. Anyone would feel the same. *I should have been doing this months ago.*

He walked to the laundry room and found Ethel folding towels. She smiled, spreading crow's feet from the corners of her eyes and deep lines around her mouth. Easily the oldest worker in his employ, she'd been working for the hotel longer than the family had lived in Tennessee. Her crinkled hands turned perfect corners. Finishing the towel, she placed it on top of the stack then grabbed another. The hot room smelled of bleach and detergent. He couldn't imagine how she had worked here every day for so many years.

"How are you doing, Mr. Sesely?" Her voice crackled, sounding even older than her age.

"I'm fine. How are you?"

She waved her hand in front of her face. "Hot. Beginning of September always seems warmer than August."

He pulled a peppermint from his pocket. It didn't seem to be a good enough gesture for a woman who'd put so many years of hard work into a place. She spied the candy and her eyes lit up. "Is that for me?"

He handed it to her. "I appreciate all you do for the hotel, Ethel."

"It's like my second home." She nudged his arm with her elbow. "Gets me away from all those bickering kids of mine for a few minutes. They're full grown. You'd think they wouldn't still fight like teenagers."

Josif knew two of Ethel's children, though in their mid-thirties, still lived with her. He was pretty sure one of them didn't even work.

She unwrapped the peppermint and popped it in her mouth. "I was craving some sugar. Thank you."

He eyed the basket of washcloths and towels she had yet to fold. "Why don't I help with those, and then you can get a few extra minutes for break?"

She smacked her lips. "I suppose I wouldn't mind the company."

He scooped out a washcloth and folded it. Surprisingly it felt good to do something besides crunch numbers and analyze data. He grabbed another and folded it as well. Within ten minutes, the laundry was neatly stacked, and Ethel was able to sit down with a cold bottle of water.

"Thanks for your help, Mr. Sesely." Her genuine appreciation warmed his heart, and he wished he hadn't spent the last few years keeping his distance from the employees.

Josif walked to his parents' apartment on the first floor and knocked on the door. He knew Mama had planned a girls' night with Sofija and Mirela. They'd had girls' nights at least two times a week. But after spending time with Ethel, he just felt he needed to give his mother a hug before she left and tell her how much she meant to him.

Papa answered the door wearing a T-shirt and Volunteers ball cap. "I'm heading over to Sofija's to pass ball with the boys. You wanna come?"

Josif would have loved to go. He'd shot hoops and passed baseballs with his dad, brother-in-law, and nephews a few times since Sabrina went to Florida. They'd had a blast together. "Wish I could, Papa, but not today. Where's Mama?"

"In the kitchen." His father waved as he pushed past him and walked down the hall.

Josif found his mother sitting at the table. She held a photograph in her hand. She looked up at him, tears glistening in her eyes. "Mama?"

"Josif, I found it."

"Found what?"

She lifted the aged Polaroid. The picture had yellowed and the colors were dull, but he could see that it was of a woman who stood in a field. She held a baby in her arm. One hand touched the crying baby's face. The woman's lips were puckered in an obvious attempt to get the baby to stop crying. He leaned closer. The woman looked like Mirela.

"It is Jovana."

Josif took the picture from his mother's grip. "Really? She looks just like Mirela."

"I told you. It is like they are twins." She took the picture back and pressed it against her chest. "I searched and searched and could not find the picture. Today I found it." She pointed to a curio cabinet. "Mirela will be so happy."

His mother was right. Mirela would be thrilled. She would pour out thanksgiving on his mother, possibly shed a few tears. And they would be genuine. She would mean them.

Just as Ethel genuinely appreciated a mere peppermint and a few minutes of help folding towels. Just as his nephews enjoyed the time they'd spent playing ball. Just as he adored his parents for all they'd done for him and his sister, and that they'd shared their love for God with them.

A sick feeling swelled in his stomach. He couldn't do it. He couldn't go to dinner with Sabrina. He would pray for her. Every day. That she would seek the peace and contentment that could only come from God. But he couldn't date her one moment longer.

He hugged his mom then headed to the hotel coffee shop. Sabrina saw him and waved. He couldn't falter or hesitate. He motioned to her, and she stepped out from behind the counter.

"Couldn't wait to see me until tonight, huh?" she simpered.

Josif shook his head as he shoved his hands in his front pants pockets. He felt guilty, like he'd wasted three years of her life. *Three years of my life, too.* Heaviness weighed on his heart. He knew Sabrina expected them to marry. One day. But he couldn't do it. He didn't want to live another day so consumed with himself and what was easiest for him. He knew as long as he and Sabrina were together that was the life he'd live. One of self-absorption. "Sabrina, I have to be honest with you."

Sabrina tensed beside him. She furrowed her eyebrows and squinted at him. "What's going on, Josif?"

"We can't see each other anymore."

She studied him for a moment as she clasped her fingers in what appeared to be an attempt to keep from strangling him. "It's Mirela, isn't it?"

Josif frowned. "No." He stepped back. "No, it isn't. It is my faith, my belief in God. . . ."

"Your faith never came between us before."

It felt as if a knife sliced through his heart. She hadn't responded in defense of her faith. She hadn't said that they shared the same relationship with their heavenly Maker. His chest ached. *God, forgive me.* "My faith should have been more evident. I'm sorry it wasn't."

She humphed. "We'll see about that."

❧

Mirela lay on her bed, holding the picture away from her so she could memorize it more thoroughly. She couldn't believe how much she looked like her mother. Even the length of her hair was the same. She brought the picture down to her chest and cradled it there. "Lord, thank You. Thank You for this gift."

Her heart had nearly burst with thanksgiving for the last several weeks. However her mom still wouldn't speak of the Sesely family. Mirela had hoped that after their lunch things would change. They hadn't, but Mirela had been able to spend several evenings with Mama Sesely and Sofija. It felt as if God had given her two families to cherish.

Ivy knocked on the door then walked into Mirela's room. She sat on the edge of the bed. "Whatcha got there?"

Mirela sat up but didn't take the picture away from her chest. "You will never believe it."

Ivy's clear blue eyes lit up and she wiggled her eyebrows. "A picture of that handsome Serbian man."

"Ivy!" Mirela laughed at her sister's dramatics. She couldn't deny she'd missed seeing Josif. He'd seemed to disappear for the last few weeks. In reality, that was good. Mirela did not want to be tempted to wish for another woman's boyfriend. Especially after she'd run into Sabrina in the hotel parking lot and the woman had told Mirela that Josif was hinting marriage. She couldn't decipher why Sabrina seemed so angry about it, but it wasn't Mirela's business, and it didn't matter anyway. She had better things to think about at the moment. Mirela shook her head. "Much better."

Ivy cocked her head and reached out her hand. "Well, show me."

Mirela held out the Polaroid. "It's my mother and me."

Ivy sucked in a deep breath. She covered her mouth with her fingertips then gingerly touched the picture. "Mirela!"

Tears pooled in Ivy's eyes, and Mirela could contain it no longer. She cried and laughed at the same time, unable to control her happiness.

Ivy wrapped her arms around her then looked at the picture again. "You look just like her, Mel."

Mirela twirled several strands of hair beside her ear and nodded. "I know."

"I mean just like her. It's amazing. It's like seeing you holding one of the babies at church."

Mirela sucked in a sob. "I know."

Ivy tucked her feet under her. "Mrs. Sesely had it?"

"She'd been looking for it. She didn't want to tell me until she found it." Mirela grabbed her sister in another hug. "You will always be my sister, and Mom and Dad will always be my parents, but I am finally learning of my past. I can't. . .I don't know how to describe how I feel."

Ivy smacked her hands on the bed. "We need to celebrate."

"How?"

"Let's go shopping."

Mirela laughed. "Ivy, you always want to go shopping."

Ivy bit her bottom lip. She grabbed the bulk of her long blond hair and wrapped it around her hand as she gazed up at the ceiling. "Won't work. I don't get paid for another week." She bounced and clapped her hands. "I know. Do you still have your gift certificate to the nail salon? I still have mine. We can go get manicures."

Mirela wrinkled her nose. "You know I don't like to get my nails fixed."

Ivy grinned like a Cheshire cat. "But you do like pedicures."

Mirela curled her toes. She couldn't deny that. She loved the hot water jetting over her feet, the warmed towel against her legs, and the fresh coat of polish on her toes. The last time they'd gotten pedicures, Ivy'd even convinced her to allow them to design her big toenails with flowers.

Ivy furrowed her brows. "Did you just hear something?"

Mirela sat still and listened. A light sniffle came from outside the door. Mirela's smile fell as she walked out of the room and spied her mother's bedroom door shut. She knocked lightly. "Mom, can I come in?"

"Not right now, Mirela."

Mirela could tell her mother tried to mask her crying. She looked at her sister, and Ivy shrugged and mouthed, "I don't know what to do."

Mirela'd been trying to understand her mom's perspective for the last few weeks. Her mother wouldn't open up as to what about the Seselys upset her so much. Mirela could only assume that her mom felt as if Mirela didn't appreciate the life she'd had. But Mirela had loved her life. She adored her family. She pressed her mouth against the crack of the door. "Mom, I love you."

Her mom sniffed. "Honey, I know you do. I love you, too."

Ivy grabbed Mirela's arm and pulled her away from the door and toward the kitchen. "Don't feel guilty, Mel. She knows you love her. Something about this upsets her, but I can't put my finger on it. Your adoption has been very open." Ivy flipped a strand of long blond hair. "And apparent."

Mirela forced a smile. She looked nothing like her adopted parents, and the family had been open about Mirela's culture. Her mom and dad had been missionaries in Serbia for years. They loved the Serbian people. But something about Mirela's learning the details of her past had her mom in a state of fits. Mirela blew out a long breath. "I wish she'd just tell me why she's so upset."

"We'll just keep praying."

Mirela nodded. She thought of the childhood tune about making new friends but keeping the old. She enjoyed her new relationship with the Seselys, but her bond with her mom was golden, and she couldn't lose it. Though it tore at her heart, she would have to focus on her mom for a little while.

ten

Josif took a bite of his mustard and onion smothered hot dog then wiped his mouth with the back of his hand. It was the second half of the Vols' game against Kentucky, and Tennessee was up 28 to 14. He picked up his soft drink and took a long swig. There was nothing better than eating junk food and cheering on his favorite college team in perfect 55-degree weather.

His brother-in-law elbowed him then pointed toward the end of the field. "We're going to score again."

The quarterback handed the ball to the running back. He ran. Ten yards to touchdown. Five. Josif and Matt jumped up and threw their hands in the air. They turned toward each other and chest bumped. "Touchdown!"

After several more whoops, Josif sat down, scooped his cup off the ground, and took another drink.

Matt nudged him. "Thanks for inviting me, man. It's been a great game. Kentucky came out looking good." He wiggled his eyebrows. "But the Vols came back. As always." He pumped his fist and yelled toward the field. "Yeah!"

"No problem."

Josif didn't mention that he'd asked Mirela first. After their conversation at the Chinese restaurant, he'd thought she would say yes. He could have sworn he'd heard excitement in her voice when he said he wanted to take her, but she'd declined, saying she had work she had to complete tonight. And he was still bummed about it.

Matt leaned over. "I'm surprised Sabrina let you invite me."

Josif mulled the comment around in his mind. Did his family think Sabrina decided his plans for him? He thought of the many times he'd eaten Indian food, which he hated. The horror movies, which he despised. He remembered the boys' football games he'd missed because Sabrina made other plans. They hadn't even gone to Chloe's ballet recital.

Sabrina had run his life, but he couldn't put his finger on when it had started and why he'd allowed it to happen. *It's because I was so busy working on the hotel. I put everything on the back burner and just let Sabrina decide.*

There would be no more of that. He'd enjoyed the time he'd spent with his family. He'd even gotten a few projects completed around his house. Most importantly, he discovered how much he'd missed his relationship with God.

He looked at Matt. "Sabrina and I broke up."

Matt raised his eyebrows. "No way."

Josif nodded. "Yep."

"Smart move." Matt held up his fist, and Josif fist bumped it. "It would have been a rough life for you, always having to do everything that woman said."

Josif didn't respond. Part of him felt defensive that Matt would talk that way about Sabrina. Josif had cared about her for three years, and even now he prayed daily that she would come to know the Lord as her Savior. If anyone had been wrong in the relationship, it had been him. He was the one not living the life he should have lived.

"I'm surprised you didn't already know. I told Papa and he must've told Mama. He tells her everything, and she tells Sofija, and I'm sure Sofija tells you. . . ."

Matt lifted his hand. "I know how the family works." He chuckled. "I've been super busy at work. Sofija probably just hasn't had a chance to tell me." He nudged Josif with his elbow. "So is Mama still matchmaking?"

"Surprisingly, she hasn't mentioned it anymore to me." *Hopefully, she isn't driving Mirela crazy. Maybe that's why she said no to the game. Maybe Mama's pushing too hard.*

Within minutes the game ended. Matt said, "I'm going to head to the bathroom before we get out of here." He snapped his fingers. "And I promised the kids I'd get them a souvenir."

"I'll wait here until the crowd thins a bit."

Matt nodded and headed out with the crowd.

Josif pulled his phone out of his front pocket to see if he'd missed any calls during the game. He hadn't, but he saw the last number he'd called. Mirela's. It looked like he'd dialed it during the game. *I must have accidently pushed the button. Maybe I should call her and apologize.*

The thought tempted him. He would have a valid excuse for calling, and it would give him the opportunity to hear her voice again. Before he could talk himself out of it, he pushed the CALL button.

The phone rang and then rang again and then again. He was about to hang up when her voice sounded on the line. "Hi, Josif."

"Hi, Mirella." He frowned. How had she known it was him? He smacked his forehead with his hand. Caller ID. Plus he'd called her earlier.

"How was the game?"

"Good. We won, 35 to 14."

"I know. I watched it." She began to stutter. "I mean, I—I watched it while I, um, got some of my—my work done."

Josif's heart sank. She wasn't telling him the full truth. She may have had things to do at home, but they weren't the reason she wouldn't go to the game with him. The rejection cut more than he expected. He'd wanted to spend time with her. To get to know her better. But he wouldn't beg her to go out with him either. He cleared his throat. "I just thought I'd tell you the score since you were busy tonight."

"Josif, I—"

He didn't let her finish. "I'll talk to you later."

He hung up before she could respond again. The crowd had cleared, so he made his way out of the stadium. He spied Matt buying T-shirts from a vendor. Matt held one up. "This is an awesome deal. Three for fifteen."

Josif nodded. He really wanted to head home. It had been a great game. He had had a good time with his brother-in-law, but the hurt from Mirela's rejection still rubbed him a little raw. He just wanted to take a long, hot shower, put on an old T-shirt and shorts, and veg in front of his television. Maybe watch the game again since he'd DVR'd it. But what he really wanted was to not feel quite so embarrassed and ditched.

❧

Mirela dragged into the day care center. She was late. She was never late. She hadn't slept for two nights.

"I'm sorry, Mrs. Jones." Mirela walked into the nursery and hung her sweater over a chair.

"That's all right. Everyone has a bad morning sometimes."

Mirela didn't know what else to say as her boss walked out the door. It was humiliating that she'd overslept because she'd tossed and turned all night. She felt like such a heel, lying to Josif about the game. But what was she supposed to say to him? Why are you asking me to a ball game when you have a girlfriend?

That's exactly what I should have said to him.

Sometimes she was just plain frustrated with her lack of

a backbone. She hadn't imagined him to be the kind of guy who would cheat on his girlfriend, but then maybe he had only wanted to go as friends. Maybe he thought of her as a sister since his mother treated her as if she were her own child.

She gagged at the thought of it. She was attracted to a man who viewed her as his sister. And who had a girlfriend. Possibly fiancée by now, if Sabrina's hunch was right. She shook her head as she picked Benny up out of his bouncy seat. He smiled at her as she puckered at him and said, "Miss Mirella is going crazy, isn't she, Benny? She's absolutely losing her mind."

Benny cackled, and Mirela blew bubbles on his belly. She played with the other babies' toes then laid Benny on the ground so she could get their morning rice cereal ready.

Cheryl opened the top of the Dutch door. "Mirela, can you watch my kids a minute?"

Mirela turned around and saw Cheryl holding her cell phone. If Mirela agreed to watch the two-year-olds, the babies would never get their breakfast. Mustering up her courage, she shook her head. "I'm sorry, Cheryl. I was late this morning and I've got to feed the babies."

Cheryl huffed. "It's not my fault you were late this morning."

Mirela took a deep breath, praying God would give her the right words. *God, I don't want to be a doormat, but I do want to be a good witness.* "You're right. It's my fault I was late, but I still have to feed the babies."

Cheryl leaned over the door and hissed. "I'll only be gone a minute." She held up her phone. "I need to take this call."

Mirela shook her head. "I'm sorry. Not right now. Once I've finished their breakfast I can help you, but only if it doesn't interfere with their schedule."

Cheryl scowled at her for several seconds before she finally shut the door. Mirela exhaled a long breath. She was terrible with confrontation. She avoided it at all costs. Almost all costs. She'd stood up to Cheryl today. Not to make her own life easier, but because the babies needed her undivided attention.

She heard the other door in the two-year-old room open. She could hear Cheryl in not-so-hushed tones, complaining to Hannah that she wouldn't help. Mirela couldn't hear Hannah's response, but she knew the three-year-olds' teacher wanted Cheryl to be more responsible for her children.

It hurt to hear some of the things Cheryl said. Mirela had helped her on more occasions than she could count. She refused for the first time for the sake of her babies' breakfast, and Cheryl slammed her. *Because I wasn't being a witness to her as I'd hoped. I was being a doormat, and she was taking advantage of me.*

As she added water to the rice cereal bowls, she asked God for wisdom and strength to confront people when necessary. Her cell phone rang in her pocket and she jumped, almost knocking over all three bowls of cereal. She pulled it out and saw her mother's name. Her heart skipped. Her mom never called her at work. She pushed the TALK button. "Mom?"

Her mother's excited voice poured over the line. "Mirela, I need you to ask off next week."

"What? Is everything all right?"

"Of course, everything is all right. I won the cruise-for-two in the hospital's employee drawing. Of course, I'll have to pay for one ticket so that all three of us can go, but three for the price of one is worth it, wouldn't you say?"

Mirela tried to process what her mother was saying. "But—"

"I told you about this. I never dreamed I'd win, but I know I told you about it. You girls have gotten so big, and it's such a wonderful vacation to the Caribbean. Ivy is asking off."

Mirela vaguely remembered her mother mentioning the drawing a few weeks ago. "When are we supposed to leave?"

"This Saturday. You'll need all of next week off."

Mirela inwardly groaned. On the day that she was late to work she'd have to ask Mrs. Jones for a week off with only one week's notice. But she'd do it. Her mom needed this trip. The five-year anniversary of her father's death was the next week. It would be good for the three of them to spend the time together. "Okay, Mom. I'll ask."

Her mother squealed. "Mirela, I can't wait. The three of us will have to go shopping this week. I haven't bought a bathing suit in years. Ugh." She laughed. "I hate to see what I'll look like in one."

Mirela smiled into the phone at her mother's excitement. She hadn't heard her that giddy since before her father passed away. "Mom, you'll look terrific."

Mirela said good-bye, clicked off her cell phone, then fed the babies. Her stomach churned, knowing she'd need to talk to Mrs. Jones today. They had several ladies on a sub list, but it was often hard to get any of them to work an entire week.

Knowing she needed to give Mrs. Jones as much notice as possible, she called the older woman and asked if she could stop by the nursery for a minute.

Concern etched Mrs. Jones's face when she walked into the room. "Mirela, what's wrong?" She looked at the three babies. "Is everyone okay?"

Mirela took a deep breath and explained about her mother's trip and her need to have the following week off.

Mrs. Jones clasped her hands in front of her. "Mirela, how

long have you worked here?"

Mirela wanted to cry. It appeared Mrs. Jones was going to remind her of the center's policy of requesting vacation time at least one month prior to the date. "Three years."

The older woman pursed her lips and paced the floor. "Well, to my recollection you have never taken a full vacation." She walked up to Mirela and patted her back. "And I'd say it's high time you do."

Mirela let out a deep breath and grinned at her boss.

The older woman winked. "I got you, didn't I?"

Mirela crinkled her nose and nodded. "You got me good."

Mrs. Jones patted her arm. "You're a good employee, Mirela. Administrators like to keep their good employees happy. Of course, you can go with your mother and sister on the cruise." She snapped her fingers. "I wish I could go with you."

As Mrs. Jones walked out the door, Mirela looked up at the ceiling. *Thanks, God. For such a rough start, You've sure made the day a lot easier.*

eleven

Josif walked out to the courtyard of the hotel. He approached one of the maintenance workers to ask about the fall flowers his mother had requested. He feared Mama's choices might need a little altering. It had been weeks since Mirela visited, and he knew Mama missed her desperately.

"Josif, I haven't seen you in weeks."

Sabrina's voice came from behind him. He turned and smiled at her. It had been awhile since they'd seen each other

"How is the new job?" Josif asked. She'd requested and been awarded a change of location with the franchise she worked for. Though he hadn't seen her, she had been at the top of his prayers. Still, he'd been surprised at how little he'd missed her.

She pushed a long strand of hair behind her shoulder. "It's terrific. The people are super easy to work with."

Josif knew she implied his family had been difficult, but he also knew that wasn't true. Sabrina's negative attitude caused the tension. Seeing her now didn't bring an ache that probably should have been there after a breakup with someone he'd dated for so long. *God, how could I have been so blind as to how superficial our relationship had become?*

Taking in her lifted chin, arched back, and the challenging gleam in her eye, Josif realized the stance was an act, an attempt to cover up the true insecurity she felt. He needed to pray even more than he had been. Compassion for her filled him. "How are you?"

His tone was more emphatic than he'd expected, and a moment of vulnerability flooded her face. The moment ended and she regained her facade of confidence and arrogance. She placed her hand on his chest and batted her eyelashes. "I'm fine."

Her flirtation stumped him. She hadn't called him a single time since he'd dissolved the relationship. He'd taken it as a sign that she agreed with the need to part ways.

She tugged on the collar of his shirt. "How's Mirela?"

He slightly lifted his chin. So that's what was going on. Sabrina still thought he'd broken up with her because of Mirela. Which was partly true, but she wasn't the biggest reason. He spread both hands upward and shrugged. "I don't know. She hasn't been around for a while."

Mirela had explained to his family that she needed to spend some time with her mom and Ivy. She hadn't gone into details, but he assumed, by the cold response they'd received initially from her adopted mother, that Mrs. Adams was the reason for the space. He didn't understand why the woman would be upset about Mirela becoming a part of their lives, but he also had no experience with adoption.

Oddly enough, though he'd known Mirela only a short time, he found he missed seeing her more than he would have expected. He thought of her every time he passed the conference room. He recalled her eyes lighting up with merriment when she first met and hugged his mother in that room. He remembered her attempt to hide her dislike for the Serbian food the night they'd finally ditched the homeland cuisine and headed out for Chinese. He missed her soft laugh, and the way it seemed to melt away all his frustrations from the day. *God, I have missed Mirela.*

"Well, I'm sure she's doing just fine." Sabrina's voice broke

Josif from his reverie. She rocked back and forth, shifting her weight from one foot to the other.

Josif realized she sported a bit more *bling*, as she called it, than she used to. A long rhinestone necklace hung to her waist. Matching earrings adorned her lobes. The heels of her black shoes were covered in rhinestones. Actually he remembered those shoes. They were the ones she'd worn the day his family met Mirela. Her makeup was a bit darker also. *God, she isn't the kind of woman I want at all. Was I blind or has she totally changed?*

Sabrina raked her hand through her hair then flipped her tresses around her shoulder. "I have a date tonight."

Josif stepped back at her declaration. Was she trying to make him jealous? He chewed the thought around in his head. Should he be jealous? He furrowed his eyebrows. He wasn't. He genuinely wanted Sabrina to be happy.

"That's terrific. I hope you have a great time."

Her expression told him that was not the reaction she'd expected. She turned and stared toward the hotel then she looked back at him, a sinister grin spreading her lips.

She wrapped her arms around him. Before he had time to respond, she pressed her lips against his cheek. She wrapped one hand around his head and whispered, "Guess this is good-bye then."

Then she rustled his hair and pushed away from him. Confused, he watched as she walked across the courtyard and into the parking lot. He had no idea what had come over her.

⁂

Mirela's cheeks warmed and her heart plummeted into her stomach as she watched Josif and Sabrina embrace on the hotel's courtyard. She hadn't seen the man in weeks. She, Ivy, and her mom had vacationed on the cruise and then she'd stayed close to home due to the five-year anniversary of her dad's death. She'd tried to keep her thoughts away from Josif Sesely, even though he seemed determined to haunt her day and night.

But to see them hug and Sabrina kiss his cheek in such a possessive manner. Mirela had never known true jealousy until that moment. She wanted to stomp onto that courtyard and demand Sabrina keep her hands off Josif.

She huffed. She imagined Josif would laugh in her face and tell the Miss Plain Jane to find a different man to dream about every waking and sleeping moment of the day. She peered down at her bright red toenails and the little white flower that had been painted on each big toenail. She should have waited to get the pedicure until *after* the visit. She had a feeling she'd want some pampering by the time she left the hotel.

With a sigh, she headed down the hall to Mama and Papa Sesely's apartment. She anticipated they'd be as happy to see her as she would them. She knocked on the door and the older woman opened it and squealed. Wrapped in a bear hug, Mirela shuffled into the apartment. Before Mama Sesely had released her, Papa had embraced both of them.

"Mirela, it is so good to see you," said Mama Sesely.

"We missed you, dear." Papa Sesely squeezed her cheek.

"I've missed you as well."

The older woman motioned her into the living area. "Come. Tell us how your vacation was."

Mirela followed them into the living room and sat on the sofa. "I brought pictures." She pulled them out of her purse and they plopped down at each side of her. They oohed and aahed over each one, especially enjoying the goofy-faced picture her family had had taken beside a plastic shark.

The door opened and Josif stepped inside. Her heart crashed against her lungs when she saw the man so close. A flash of something raced through his eyes. Longing? No, it couldn't be. He lifted his hand and she knew he was about to scratch the stubble on his jaw. When he did just as she thought, she inwardly whined. *God, how could I possibly have paid such close attention to this man? And why is he nervous? He only does that when he's nervous.*

The thought tripped her up as she studied him, wishing she could read his mind.

"Mirela." He masked his thoughts with a full smile. "It's been a long time."

"It's been almost three weeks. Nineteen days," said Mama Sesely.

Papa nudged her with his elbow. "Not that she's counting."

Mirela laughed but she couldn't tear her gaze from Josif for long. His hair was a bit longer than she remembered. She wondered if he simply needed a cut or if he was growing it out a bit. The curls at the nape of his neck were adorable, and she imagined touching one of them. Heat warmed her face and she looked away for a moment. Peeking back at him, she realized he was also tanner than the last time she'd seen him. He must be working outside more, instead of constantly stuck in his office.

"So, what brings you over here?"

Mirela snapped out of her dreamland and clapped her hands together. She looked at Mama Sesely. "Actually, I'd like to ask you a favor."

The older woman sat up and nodded. "Anything, dear."

Mirela bit her bottom lip. "I need to raise a bit more money for the shoeboxes, and I wondered if you and Sofija would be willing to help me with a bake sale."

Mama Sesely clapped. "Of course, we would help you." She patted Mirela's arm as she stood and shuffled to the kitchen. "I will get my cookbooks to decide on which desserts. You will come here, and we will use the hotel kitchen during the morning since we don't offer a hot breakfast. Some of the staff will be there but we'll just stay out of their way." She motioned to Papa Sesely. "Come help me find my recipes."

Papa rolled his eyes, but he stood and followed his wife into the kitchen. Mirela exhaled a long breath when she and Josif were left alone in the living room. She tried not to look at him, but she noticed when he crossed his legs, placing his foot on his knee, then picked at his shoelaces. He cleared his throat, and she again wondered why he seemed as nervous as she.

"You've made Mama's day by asking her to help you."

Mirela glanced at Josif. "It's made mine just to see her again."

Silence draped over them, and Mirela picked at her fingernails. She couldn't imagine how it could take so long to find cookbooks. She wanted to experience the easy camaraderie she'd shared with Josif when they'd had dinner at the Chinese restaurant, but her feelings for him had changed since then. Deepened. She'd missed him. At moments, she'd needed so desperately to see him. She couldn't make small talk with him now. She wanted him as more than a friend, but she wouldn't consider trying to take someone else's boyfriend. *Of three years!*

For all she knew they'd gotten engaged over the last few weeks. Bile rose in her throat at the thought. Mama and Papa Sesely needed to hurry up. If they didn't, she'd have to haul herself into that kitchen and drag them out. When Mirela thought she would burst, Mama Sesely walked back in the room, holding two large books.

She looked at Josif and clucked her tongue. "Why are you not talking with Mirela? After all, she is your future wife."

Mirela gaped at the older woman. Had she misunderstood what Mama Sesely just said? Mirela sneaked a peek at Josif. His face had already blossomed into a bright red shade. No. She'd understood. But why would she have said that? *Dear Lord, surely my attraction is not so evident. I have tried to battle it.*

"Mama." Josif's voice sounded low and disapproving. It was obvious their future matrimony was not his idea, which only deepened Mirela's humiliation.

Mama Sesely swatted the air with her hands. "Now is not the time to discuss." She pointed to the cookbooks. "Time to pick desserts."

Mirela bit her bottom lip, willing away the tears that threatened to swell up when she was embarrassed. What would have made Mama Sesely refer to Mirela as Josif's "future wife"?

twelve

Josif could hear laughter coming from the kitchen. Mama, Sofija, and Mirela were making desserts for the bake sale to raise money for the shoebox ministry. He'd had a hard time focusing on paperwork the entire morning. He knew it had something to do with knowing a long, dark-haired beauty, whose face kept him awake at night, was only a few rooms away from him.

He chuckled when he remembered her expression a few days ago when Mama had burst into the room, announcing Mirela as his future wife. Obviously Mama hadn't shared the plan with Mirela before then. The poor young woman looked as if she'd been sucker punched. Her cheeks burned crimson, and she'd spent the rest of the visit stumbling over every word she said.

After shoving the paperwork he still needed to finish into his to-do tray, he stood and stretched. He could sit there no longer. Looking in the mirror his sister had hung on the wall, because she said it made the room look larger, he checked to make sure his hair wasn't standing on its end, as he sometimes mussed his hair as he worked. With everything in place, he walked out of the office and toward the kitchen.

The women had been working for hours and had the desserts to prove it. Trays of cookies and cupcakes lined one side of the kitchen. He spied several pies on another counter. If his nose still worked as it should, he knew some of those pies were apple, his favorite.

"You will do a wonderful job making *krofne*." His mother patted Mirela's hand.

Using the back of her hand, Mirela swiped a strand of hair away from her face. Flour dotted her cheek and chin. Unlike his mother and sister who had no outward appearances of having been baking, Mirela's apron was covered with finger smears of white and brown ingredients. Josif wondered how much time Mirela spent baking. Probably very little.

"But the directions are so precise, and the doughnuts you made tasted so delicious. I don't want to mess them up." Mirela pointed to the trash can, brimming with several burnt items. *She must have messed a few things up.*

His mother swatted the air. "Nonsense. We do not learn if we do not try. And when we try, sometimes we make mistakes and have to start over. It is part of the learning."

Josif watched as Mirela inhaled and then exhaled a deep breath. The pitiful expression on her face drew him, and he stepped into the kitchen. "Would you like some help? It smells too good in here for me to stay cooped up in my office."

Sofija rolled the homemade pie dough. "You wanting a taste test, little brother?"

"Maybe later." Josif grinned as he walked toward Mirela and Mama. Mirela didn't make eye contact with him but simply wrung her hands together. He wondered if she was still embarrassed at his mother's outburst during Mirela's last visit, regarding their "upcoming" nuptials. *As long as she is intrigued by the idea and not repulsed by it.* It would break his heart if the notion disgusted her entirely.

She sneaked a peek up at him, and he saw a hint of pink

in her cheeks. She wasn't repulsed by it. She was attracted to him. He knew she was. She had to be. *So why is she still acting shy around me? Am I giving the wrong signals?* He cleared his throat. "I've always wanted to learn how to make Serbian doughnuts."

Mama squinted at him. She knew him too well. He feared she would see through the charade and blurt out that she knew he only wanted to spend time with Mirella. Instead, she said, "You have always wanted to know how to make krofne?"

"If I make them half as good as you, they will be mouthwatering."

Mama continued to study him. Finally she smacked her hand against her hip. "All right. Help Mirela. Let's get started."

Mirela was more nervous than he'd expected. Her hands shook as she measured the sugar and poured it into the scalded milk and butter. Then, if he hadn't stopped her, she would have added an extra teaspoon of salt. He wasn't a cook, but he was pretty sure an extra teaspoon of salt would have seriously altered the taste.

"Check the water's temperature, Josif," Mama commanded.

He stuck a thermometer in the water. Once it reached 110 degrees, he nodded to Mirela and she poured in the yeast. While Mama went to the refrigerator to get the eggs, Josif leaned toward Mirela and whispered, "I think we're doing a great job."

Mirela stiffened and simply nodded. He wanted to talk with the woman whose company he'd enjoyed at the restaurant the first night they met or the one he'd enjoyed Chinese with a week later. He didn't know what to think of the aloof Mirella he'd encountered the last few times he'd seen her. *She's definitely not a natural baker. She's probably just nervous about the doughnuts.*

Josif went back to work, adding the milk and yeast mixture to a large bowl. Mirela added the eggs and started to mix the ingredients while he added flour as she stirred. Once they finished mixing, they covered the dough to allow it time to rise. He clapped his hands together and looked at his mother. "Now what can I do to help while we wait?"

Mama pointed at the cookies. "Why don't you and Mirela bag the cookies? Three to a bag."

Mirela nodded and walked toward the counter. He followed her. He knew she talked more than this. Maybe she just felt uncomfortable in front of his mother and sister. *Or maybe she really doesn't want to have anything to do with me.* The thought stabbed at his heart. He prayed that wasn't the reason for her awkwardness. If he could just have a little bit of time alone with her, get her to acknowledge they were in the same room, he'd ask her straight-out what was going on.

"I've got to take a break and check on the boys!" Sofija called from the other side of the kitchen.

"Good idea. I'm going to go check on Papa," his mother said. She turned and winked at Josif. He knew Mirela saw her as Mirela turned around abruptly.

He groaned inwardly. Sometimes he didn't know what to do with his family. He picked up a baggie, placed three cookies inside it, then sealed it shut. Mirela did the same. She didn't speak, and he fought himself about what to say to her. He was getting the chance he'd asked for, and he couldn't form a single complete thought in his mind. The silence grew like fungus in an untreated swimming pool.

He placed another baggie of cookies in their "finished"

pile. This was silly. He was a grown man. Thirty years old. He had no reason to be nervous about talking to a woman. *Especially his "future wife."* Mama's words pierced his mind, and he rolled his eyes. He didn't need to be thinking brides. He needed to think dates. "Mama and Sofija are enjoying helping with the bake sale."

"I couldn't have done it without them."

"I bet you'll raise tons of money off these desserts."

Even though she continued to focus on filling baggies, he saw the twinkle that lit her eyes. "I'm sure we will. Have you tasted some of these foods?"

He nodded. "Several times. How much money are we trying to raise?"

"A thousand dollars. It seems like so much." Mirela looked up and smiled at him. "But with your mother's baking, I think we won't have any trouble."

The tension seemed to escape her body as she chatted about past fund-raisers and donations, and what she needed and prayed for to finish raising the money for one thousand shoeboxes. Her zeal drew him, and he found himself wanting to do anything he could to help her meet, or even exceed, her goal.

She sealed the last baggie of cookies then crossed her arms in front of her chest. He watched as she drank in the mound of confections they'd created. "I can't believe everything we've baked this morning."

"Sounds like you deserve a break. Why don't you let me take you to lunch?"

He didn't think before the words slipped from his lips. He should have mulled over how he wanted to ask her, should have come up with a way that showed her he was interested in her, not just trying to feed her stomach. He wanted to take her to lunch. He wanted to take her to dinner and a movie.

But the expression on her face made him wish he'd kept the thought to himself. For the blink of a second, she appeared as if she'd say yes, then her expression clouded and she shook her head. "Excuse me, Josif. I need to. . .need to. . .I need to go to the restroom."

Without looking back, she raced out of the room. Josif furrowed his eyebrows. What had happened? She'd let down her guard and they'd had fun fixing cookie baggies. He grunted as he strode back to his office, deflated and rejected. He had work to do anyway. He should have never left his office.

❧

Mirela could not believe Josif had asked her to lunch. She tapped the top of the steering wheel as she waited at the red light. *What kind of man asks a woman out to lunch when he has a girlfriend?*

She pressed the gas pedal when the light changed to green. Exhaling a deep breath, she knew her emotions were in overdrive, that she was more sensitive than she should be, that she was overreacting.

Josif most likely didn't mean it as a date, but simply a sharing of a meal with a friend after they'd been working together. No doubt he thought her response was ridiculous. *He's probably sitting in his office right now, wondering what in the world would have caused me to respond in such a way. "I need to go to the restroom"?* She smacked her forehead. *Why did I say that?*

If she weren't so attracted to the man, she wouldn't have acted so foolishly. She'd shared lunch with men from church after working on a project together. It was true; she never went to lunch alone with married men for the sake of appearances and temptation, even if there was no apparent attraction. She never wanted to do anything to give Satan a foothold. And Josif had a girlfriend, a long-time girlfriend, and it didn't feel right to go to lunch with him.

Even if you've gone twice before?

Mirela gripped the steering wheel as an inner battle waged inside her mind. *And now I'm attracted to him, thinking about him all the time. Which proves my point about why I never eat alone with married men. Temptation!*

But he's not married, and Sabrina's not right for him.

Who's to say she's not right for him? It's not my place, and I shouldn't be thinking about him.

The fight in her mind continued to rage as she pulled into the driveway and then yanked the car into PARK. She stormed into the house, frustrated with the warring thoughts in her mind. She'd always been sensible and even-tempered. Until now. Now she felt like a tilt-a-whirl had taken up residence in her head, causing her thoughts and emotions to sway one way, then another.

"Hey Mirela. I'm glad you're home." Ivy's voice sounded from the dining room. "Come help me fold laundry."

Mirela glanced around at the dusted and swept living area. Several church members were coming over after work the next day to help pack shoeboxes. With Mom working at the hospital today, Ivy'd had to clean the house by herself. Guilt rushed through Mirela as she walked into the dining room and spied the mound of clean clothes on the table. "I'm sorry I wasn't here to help."

Ivy swatted her hand. "Nonsense. You were making stuff for the bake sale. How'd it go?"

Mirela forced a smile as she picked up a towel and folded

it. "Great. We fixed more cookies, cupcakes, pies, and Serbian doughnuts than I've ever seen. And they wouldn't let me pay for the ingredients."

"That's really nice of them."

Mirela scooped up one of Ivy's T-shirts, folded it, then placed it in her pile. Josif's request to take her to lunch flooded her mind. He'd looked so hurt when she'd refused. More wounded than he should have looked when he had a girlfriend who was probably running around the hotel somewhere. She grabbed another towel and folded it with gusto.

"So that's all you've got to tell me?"

Mirela looked at her sister. Ivy smirked and Mirela inwardly growled. "There's nothing else to tell."

"Really?"

Mirela wrinkled her nose. She'd never been a good liar, and she especially couldn't lie to Ivy. Her sister knew she was fibbing even before the actual words came out. Mirela huffed. "Josif asked to take me to lunch."

"So?"

Mirela shot a look at Ivy. "He has a girlfriend."

"Maybe they broke up."

"When I walked in, she had her arms around him, and then she kissed his cheek."

Ivy frowned. "Oh." She picked up a washcloth and folded it. "Maybe he didn't mean anything by the invitation. He was just offering to feed you after working all morning."

"I know." Mirela rubbed her temples with the tips of her fingers. "I just feel like he acts like. . . Why does he have to be so nice?"

"And so cute."

"You're not helping."

"Sorry."

Mirela looked at Ivy. She couldn't help but smile at the teasing expression on her sister's face. Mirela's phone beeped, and she pulled it out of her front jeans' pocket. "I have a voicemail. I didn't even know I'd gotten a call."

"Maybe it's a tall, dark, and handsome Serbian."

"Ivy!" Mirela swatted her with a washcloth and Ivy shrugged away laughing.

She pressed the button to listen to the voicemail. To her surprise it was Cheryl asking Mirela to return her call. She sounded upset. Mirela pulled the phone away from her ear. Cheryl had never called her before. All the workers had each other's numbers for emergencies at work, but she and Cheryl never talked outside of the day care.

She looked at Ivy. "That's odd. It was Cheryl."

"From work?"

"Yeah."

"Isn't she the one who drives you crazy?"

"Yes." She searched her phone's memory for Cheryl's number. Once she found it, she lifted her index finger. "I'll be back in a minute."

Mirela walked into the living area while Cheryl's phone rang. She finally answered. "Hello." Cheryl still sounded as if she'd been crying.

"Cheryl, this is Mirela. Did you need me?"

"I shouldn't have called. Kyle left, and I was upset. . . ." Her voice trailed off.

Mirela tried to tamp down the frustration she usually felt when it came to her coworker. "I'm sorry. Can I help?"

"My mom's coming over." She sniffed and her voice cracked.

Something cracked in Mirela's heart as well. She prayed

for Cheryl, wanted to be kind to her, but Mirela knew her aggravation with the woman had been stronger than the care and love she should feel. A sudden need to help her rose up within Mirela. "Would you like to come over to my house tomorrow afternoon? We're packing shoeboxes. You'd enjoy it."

"Packing shoeboxes for what?"

"For Christmas presents for children in other countries—"

Cheryl interrupted her. "Oh yeah. I saw the article in the paper."

Mirela had forgotten about the article. Not only had it brought the Sesely family into her life, but her colleague who was so hardened by the world had also read it. *God, You use everything, even newspaper articles, for Your purposes.*

"So would you like to come?"

It seemed hours passed before Cheryl responded. "I might." She paused again, and Mirela wasn't sure if she should repeat her invitation or simply say good-bye. Cheryl's voice sounded again. "Thanks for calling me back, Mirela. I appreciate it."

She hung up, and Mirela felt humbled all the way down to her brightly painted toenails. Cheryl did take advantage of her, but she was a woman who didn't know the Lord, who lived stuck in the darkness of the world. Mirela needed to love her with a patience that surpassed understanding. With a patience that only God could give.

God, I pray Cheryl will come to know You as Lord and Savior. I can't believe she called me. Me? The last time we talked it had been an argument. Help me be a witness for You.

She walked back into the dining room and joined Ivy folding the clothes. "What was that all about?" asked Ivy.

"Her live-in boyfriend left her."

"That's good though, right?"

Mirela placed a hand on her chest. "I think it's good. The two of them fought constantly, and though she never came out and said it, I felt like he kept her kind of trapped. I invited her to our house tomorrow."

"You did?"

Mirela nodded. She saw the shocked expression on her sister's face. "I should have been a better witness to her before now."

Ivy wrapped her arm around Mirela's shoulder. "You are always so hard on yourself. Mirela, you're obviously a good witness to her. In her time of sadness, she called you. Doesn't that say something?"

Mirela nodded. "I hope you're right."

"Of course I'm right." Ivy pointed to the enormous piles of folded clothes. "You put those away while I get the food for tomorrow's lunch ready."

Mirela snorted. "Gladly. I don't want to touch a stove for a week."

"Baking too much for you?"

"I loved it." She showed Ivy the two places on her hand where she'd burned herself. "But I still have quite a bit to learn."

Ivy laughed as she walked out of the dining room. Mirela stared at the table. Though it had only been a week since they'd done laundry, it looked as if they had enough clothes to last a month. In her childhood, she'd been content with two sets of clothes. One to wear. The other to wash. It was all she'd known, and it had been enough.

Her heartbeat sped up with the knowledge they would begin filling shoeboxes the next day. The children in other countries would be overwhelmed with joy when they received their gifts. Just as she had rejoiced those many years ago. For many it would be the first present they'd ever received. *And, God, maybe Cheryl will come to help tomorrow. May she want the best present she could ever receive—You.*

thirteen

Josif loved Sunday afternoons. Especially during football season. He propped up his feet in his sister's recliner then grabbed his soft drink off the coaster on the end table. Sundays were even better when the Colts were playing, like today.

Sofija hollered from the kitchen. "You boys want some chips or pretzels?"

"Pizza rolls!" yelled twelve-year-old Ross.

Sofija walked into the living room, wiping wet hands on a towel. Chloe tagged behind Sofija. If Mama were here, she'd have the men's hides for letting Sofija do the dishes after she'd just fixed them lunch. But the game was starting, and he and his brother-in-law and two nephews loved the Colts. And she'd offered.

"Pizza rolls?" Sofija placed her hands on her hips. "You just ate burgers."

Ross jumped up and patted his stomach. "I'm a growing boy, Mom."

Josif laughed as Cole stood up on tiptoes in attempt to be as tall as his brother.

Matt chuckled. "Looks like we have *two* growing boys, Sofija."

Sofija shook her head. "Two boys who are going to have to get jobs because they're eating us out of house and home."

Cole scrunched up his face. "But I'm only nine."

With obviously feigned seriousness, Ross placed his hand

over his heart. "Mom, there are laws against child labor." He motioned to his brother and clucked his tongue just like Josif's Mama. "Are you really going to starve your son?"

Catching on to his brother's antics, Cole lowered his bottom lip and batted his eyelashes.

Josif and Matt burst into laughter, as Sofija rolled her eyes and lifted her hands in surrender. "Okay. Okay. Pizza rolls it is."

The commercials ended and Josif focused on the game. With only a few minutes left in the first half, he cheered when the Colts recovered a fumble and ran back within ten yards of the goal line. His nephews jumped off the floor and high-fived then chest bumped each other. Until a few weeks ago, Josif hadn't realized what big sports fans Ross and Cole were. He knew they sported jerseys and ball caps most days. He knew they played a different sport each season, but he hadn't realized how passionate they were at such young ages. *But I should have.*

The boys high-fived their dad then Josif. Guilt niggled at his gut. He'd missed a lot over the last few years. Even though the hotel thrived, he'd come to understand the time he could have spent with his family was lost forever. But it hadn't been just the hours he put in at the hotel. He'd finally admitted to himself that Sabrina had encouraged his separation from family. He'd allowed her beauty and her driven nature to succeed in overshadowing what was most important to him.

Focusing back on the game, he watched as the Colts' offense lined up against the Patriots' defense. The ball was snapped then thrown.

Josif jumped out of the recliner, lifting his hands to the ceiling. "Touchdown!"

His nephews bounced around, showing their touchdown dances while he and Matt high-fived.

"Woohoo!" Sofija said in mock excitement as she walked into the living room, holding a plate.

Josif realized his big sister had never understood the value of a football game.

After placing the pizza rolls on the coffee table, she said, "Food's ready," then headed back into the kitchen.

The boys yowled as they popped pizza rolls into their mouths. Sofija returned with bowls of chips and dips. She handed a bowl to Josif then one to Matt. Bending down, she placed a chaste kiss on Matt's lips.

A moment of jealousy flashed through Josif. He wanted what his sister and Matt had. The love they obviously shared. The children God had blessed them with. There was much more to life than hotel renovations and positive reviews. *There's a balance between hard work and working too hard, and I've teetered on the wrong side too long.*

He tried not to think about it as he watched the last minute of the game. The second half ended and the boys ran outside to pass the football for a few minutes.

"So when are you asking Mirela out?"

Josif looked at his brother-in-law then glanced around to make sure Sofija wasn't in the room. The last thing he needed was for her to listen to any conversations about Mirela. She'd run to Mama and blabber everything he said, and then Josif would hear about it nonstop.

"I asked her to lunch yesterday. She said no."

"Really?"

Josif shrugged. He didn't want his brother-in-law to know how much her rejection had niggled at him.

"She acts like she's interested in you. Every time I've

seen the two of you in the same room it's like some kind of magnet forces both of you to look at each other."

Josif wrinkled his nose. "What a corny thing to say."

"I know." Matt made a gagging sound as he stuck his index finger in his mouth. "It's those stinkin' chick flicks Sofija makes me watch. Every once in a while I say something that makes me want to barf."

Josif laughed. "Then maybe I'll just stay single."

Matt didn't respond, and Josif felt the weight of the silence in the room, even with the commercials blaring. He didn't want to be single. He wanted a woman in his life. He wanted Mirela.

"Ask her out again."

Josif looked at Matt. "I don't know. A man's gotta have his pride."

Matt humphed. "If I'd had too much pride, I'd have never gotten a date with your sister. She turned me down three times."

"She did?"

"Yeah." Matt raked his hand through his thinning hair. "I don't think she'd envisioned falling for a redhead."

"It's not all that red now."

"That's just 'cause there's less of it."

Josif chuckled as he lifted up his hands. "I was trying to take a positive spin on it."

Matt grinned. "Yeah, sure." He shoved a chip in his mouth. "Seriously though, I'm pretty sure the Bible has a few things to say about pride." He brushed his fingers together. "You should ask her again."

Josif pondered Matt's words. His brother-in-law was right. He shouldn't let his pride stop him. He'd ask her out again. The worst thing she could do was say no. Again.

Mirela hefted Benny higher on her hip. She pointed to the long folding tables lining the basement walls. "Stuffed animals are at table one. Small toys at table two. School supplies at three. Personal hygiene at four. Hard candy and gum at five. And extra items, like socks, shirts, hair ribbons, and whatnot, at table six." She turned toward the shoeboxes stacked almost to the ceiling along the far wall. "And of course, there are the shoe boxes. Do you have any questions?"

Cheryl's eyes were opened wide as she looked around the basement. "I can't believe you collected all this stuff."

Much to Mirela's surprise, Cheryl had showed up for worship at her church that morning. Mirela had invited her colleague on several occasions, but Cheryl had never attended. Until today.

Mirela patted Benny's bottom as he started to fuss. "What's amazing is how many people donate to us. Especially since the newspaper article. Last year we sent five hundred boxes. We'll have over one thousand this year."

Cheryl continued to stare at the mass of items. She looked like a deer who'd found herself planted in the middle of the road, mesmerized by the bright lights too quickly approaching. "How do I know what to put in the boxes?"

Ivy grabbed Cheryl's hand. "I'll show you."

Mirela bounced Benny as she watched Ivy guide Cheryl through filling a shoebox. Cheryl seemed awestruck by the whole thing, but she'd also acted softened somehow. It was like she was open to the ministry.

Benny continued to fuss, so Mirela scaled the steps to the main level of their home. With several church friends visiting to help fill the boxes, she hadn't planned to keep Benny today. But when she picked up the baby and his sister for Sunday school, Mirela noted the deep bags under Emily's eyes. Mirela knew the young mother did her best to keep their family going, and she'd learned firsthand that Benny wasn't always the best sleeper.

When Emily shared her need to do laundry, clean, and go to the grocery store, Mirela knew in her spirit she needed to offer to watch the kids. At first, Emily refused, but Mirela soon talked her into it.

Six-year-old Bella was downstairs, thrilled to be helping with the shoebox ministry. Benny, on the other hand, had been cantankerous all morning. Mirela changed his diaper then took a bottle from the refrigerator. Warming it in warm water in the sink, she cooed at the cranky baby. "You're going to drink your bottle and take a nice nap, so that when I take you home, you'll be in a happy mood for your mommy."

Benny whimpered, and Mirela tickled his belly. "Now we'll have no more of that."

Benny allowed a quick smile then went back to fussing. After testing the bottle, Mirela walked into the living area and sat in the rocking chair. She held Benny tight as she fed him his bottle. He splayed his fingers just below her neck and scratched at her skin. His eyelids lifted and shut, and Mirela knew he was tired. As she rocked, she hummed a hymn. Before he'd finished the bottle, his breathing deepened and he fell asleep.

Mirela pressed her head against the chair. She enjoyed rocking Benny, but she'd been so excited to fill shoeboxes. November was just around the corner. In a little over a month, she'd make the trip to Boone, North Carolina, to drop them off. All week she'd been looking forward to today. Even Cheryl had shown up. Mirela needed to be in the basement.

God, settle my frustrations. There's nothing I can do about it. She hadn't brought Benny's portable playpen, and she wouldn't lay him down somewhere and then leave him to go back to the basement. No, she was stuck upstairs, holding and rocking a baby while he slept. Something she did every day.

She let out a deep breath. *God, this wasn't how I planned this day. And I planned today well.*

She inwardly chuckled at her own thoughts. How many times had she planned something only to have God alter what took place? Her dad used to tease about God's sense of humor when it came to human plans. "Might as well let God guide the day, girls," he used to say to her and Ivy. "He's going to do it anyway."

She and her sister had always laughed at the silly way he said it, but experience taught Mirela the truth of her dad's words. She placed the half-empty bottle on the end table and nestled Benny close. She whispered, "I might as well enjoy my afternoon with you."

"You're really good at that, you know."

Mirela turned at the sound of her mother's voice. Her mom sat down on the couch beside the rocker.

"Good at what?"

"Taking care of babies. God's given you a natural way with them."

Mirela smiled at Benny. He made a sucking motion with his mouth. "I love babies."

Her mom sat forward and placed her elbows on her knees. She clasped her hands together. "I never talked with your biological mother. At least, I don't think so. It's possible I may have met her, but I never would have known that she would pass away and I would adopt her child. I worked with so many women, and you know the bulk of your dad's and my ministry was in another town."

Mirela held her breath. She longed to launch questions at her mom, to ask all she knew about her Serbian family, but she bit back the words. Her mom started to pick at her fingernails, and Mirela prayed she would continue to talk.

"When we adopted you I noticed your sister had a calming effect on babies. She'd told me your mother was the same way. She said you looked like your mother." Her mom looked at her. "I saw the picture in your room."

Mirela swallowed. She didn't know what to say. She didn't know if it hurt her mom to see a picture of Mirela's biological mother. She didn't want to hurt her, this woman she loved so fiercely. Since she was a small girl, Sarah Adams had been her mother, and to Mirela she always would be.

"You look very much like her. Jovana was her name."

Mirela nodded and reminded herself to keep taking breaths. She didn't want her mom to stop talking.

"She was a beautiful woman, and she gave me a beautiful daughter." She stood and reached for the baby. "Why don't you let me rock Benny so you can help downstairs?"

"Mom?"

Her mother shook her head as she lifted Benny off Mirela's chest. "This is hard for me. You're *my* daughter." She paused and blew out a long breath. "We've done enough talking for now. Go help downstairs."

Mirela stood, and her mother slipped into the rocking chair. Benny squirmed for a moment, and Mom patted his bottom until he settled down. "Mom?"

Sarah shushed her. "Go on, Mirela."

Mirela wanted to ask questions. What else did she know about her sister? Were some of the children she remembered sleeping with actually Mirela's own brothers or sisters, or were they her older sister's children? She studied her mom who had already pressed her head against the back of the chair and closed her eyes. It wouldn't do any good to ask her mother now.

Mirela headed toward the basement door. She turned and looked back at her mother once more. She whispered, "Looks like you have a way with babies, too."

Her mother opened her eyes and smiled. "Thank you, Mirela."

fourteen

Mirela watched as her sister shoved another Serbian doughnut in her mouth. "Mmm. These are so good. What did you say they were called again?"

"Krofne," Mama Sesely responded. "Mirela and Josif made them."

Ivy winked at Mirela. "They did?"

Mirela pursed her lips at her sister. "Mama Sesely, you and Sofija made most of them."

Sofija's son Ross and her husband hefted a long folding table off the back of their full-size truck. "Where do you want this table?" asked Matt.

Mirela pointed to the small card table she and Ivy had brought. "Beside that one."

Mirela helped Mama Sesely arrange the desserts in groups. She'd made *torta praska*, an apricot torte that Mirela had never seen before, as well as *reforma torta*, which was a walnut sponge cake with layers of chocolate filling. Mirela gasped when she realized Mama Sesely's backseat was filled with even more confections. "We'll never sell all this."

Sofija pulled a cardboard poster from the backseat of her truck. "Sure we will."

Mirela pointed to the poster. "What is that?"

She grinned. "Advertising."

Mirela read the sign: THE MOST DELICIOUS AMERICAN AND SERBIAN DESSERTS EVER MADE. Mirela surveyed the shopping center. "Where are you going to hang it?"

Sofija slowly shook her head. "We're not going to hang it. We're going to hold it up and encourage people to stop by."

Mirela choked. "Oh no."

Ivy clapped her hands. "It'll be like advertising at a car wash. I'll help hold up the sign."

It was times like these when Mirela knew, even beyond their appearances, that she and Ivy did not share genes. Mirela would never, could never, stand in front of moving vehicles and petition their passengers to come and purchase a product. Her cheeks flamed with embarrassment at the very thought of it.

"Can I go with Ivy, Mommy?" Chloe pulled at the bottom of Sofija's shirt.

Sofija pulled another sign out of the truck. "Of course you can. Mommy's going, too."

Ivy grabbed Chloe's hand. "This will be fun."

Hand in hand, the two of them skipped toward the road, with Sofija following close behind them.

Mama Sesely leaned close to Mirela. "You and I will take care of the money."

"Sounds good to me."

Matt walked toward them. "Do you need anything else?"

Mama tapped her lip then shook her head. "No. Looks like we're ready."

Matt and Ross waved good-bye, and Mirela settled into one of the fold-up chairs they'd brought. It was still early. The weather was nice, but she didn't expect any customers for a little while. She picked up her to-go cup of java and sipped it.

A slight breeze whipped through her hair. She loved the smell of fall. Even in front of a shopping center with buildings and vehicles all around her, Tennessee was the most beautiful place to be in October. In the not-so-far distance, God's majestic mountains stood, proudly boasting their multicolored trees.

Tourists flocked to the city to sneak a peek at their beauty. Mirela couldn't blame them. If heaven looked as wondrous as the Tennessee mountains that rose and fell into each other, she'd be forever awestruck. And yet she knew earth only showed a glimpse of God's glory. She couldn't fathom, couldn't even begin to wrap her mind around what heaven would be like.

Mama Sesely patted her arm, breaking her silent praise. "We have customers."

To Mirela's surprise, a van had pulled up and a young mother got out and made her way to their table. Before the woman had paid, two more women arrived, as well as an older man. People continued to flock to their tables. Each time Mirela thought they'd get a break, someone else showed up. She looked at her watch and gasped. Three hours had passed.

Sofija and Chloe approached the table. Sofija pulled her cell phone out of her pocket. "Chloe's hungry. I'm texting Matt to bring us some food."

Mirela beckoned for Ivy to come to them. Her crazy sister had been standing by the road the entire time. Mama Sesely took money from a customer. Out of the corner of her eye, Mirela saw another car pull up. Her stomach growled. She was thankful for all they'd sold, but she was growing weary and needed a break. She knew Mama Sesely had to be exhausted.

Ivy made her way to them. She dropped the sign behind the table and plopped into a chair. "I'm whipped."

Mirela pointed to Sofija. "She's going to see if Matt will

bring us some food. What do you want?"

"I think you all should take a lunch break. My treat."

Mirela turned at the familiar voice. Chloe squealed and jumped into Josif's arms. "Hi, Uncle Josif." She patted her stomach. "My belly is hungry."

"Well, then it's time to get some lunch." Josif looked at her, and Mirela felt her knees weaken. Probably just from fatigue and her hunger.

Mama Sesely frowned. "We can't leave." She pointed to a couple walking toward their table. "We still have customers."

"Mama, you need to eat," said Sofija.

Before she could respond, Matt pulled into the parking lot and parked. Seconds later he and the boys hopped out, their arms loaded with fast food. He winked at his wife then turned toward Josif. "I've got lunch for my crew. Why don't you take Mama, Ivy, and Mirela to get some lunch?"

Josif's smile looked so mischievous that she was sure he and his brother-in-law had planned it. But why? Mirela knew Mama Sesely was diabetic and needed to eat at regular intervals, but Mirela and Ivy could stay. She pursed her lips as she realized their reasoning. Josif's mother would never leave all of them to get some lunch. She turned toward Mama Sesely. "It sounds like a good idea."

She sneaked a peek at Josif. He smiled at her in a way she didn't understand, didn't want to try to understand. She looked back at his mother. "The temperature is nice, but the sun has been beating down on us all day. We need to take a break."

Mama Sesely straightened her shoulders. "I'm fine."

Ivy hopped to her feet. "I'm starving."

Mirela touched Mama Sesely's arm. "I'm hungry, too, and I won't be able to eat a bite of food if I know you're still standing out here in the hot sun." She'd said the right words. The woman let out a quick breath and nodded. "Fine. We'll go eat."

Mirela followed Mama Sesely to Josif's car. He stepped up beside Mirela and touched her elbow. She flinched and he pulled his hand away. She looked up at him, and he half grinned as he raked his fingers through his hair. His voice sounded hesitant. "I may need to recruit your help more often. Mama seems to listen to you."

Mirela nodded as she slid into the backseat beside her sister. He sounded adorable when he was nervous. A part of her wished she hadn't startled at his touch. The other part of her, the part that had sense, focused on the scenery outside her window. She would not show any attraction for Josif.

❧

Josif took them to his mother's favorite buffet restaurant. He knew if he took her there, Mama would allow herself to take her time to eat. With each of them getting up to get their own food, Josif also hoped it would give him the opportunity to ask Mirela on a date. A real date. Movie and dinner or whatever she wished. Not just lunch.

Once the waitress took their drink order, Mama grabbed up her plate and headed for the buffet. Josif waited a moment, hoping that Ivy would follow his mother and Mirela would pause long enough that he could talk to her alone. Instead Mirela picked up her plate and followed after his mom.

He let out his breath as he took his own plate and filled it up with sliced beef, gravy, mashed potatoes, green beans, and a sourdough roll. Though he had a smorgasbord of options, he tended to stick to his usual fare at this buffet. Occasionally he'd get back up for some fried okra, but today he just wanted to stay planted in his seat and wait for a moment of opportunity when Ivy and his mother left the table at the same time.

He sat back down before any of the women returned. He dragged his fork through the mashed potatoes. He couldn't eat until they returned. They'd need to pray together. He didn't really want to eat anyway. His stomach was a rolling ball of nerves. Maybe he should have told Ivy his plan. Though he wasn't positive, he thought she would want Mirela to go out with him.

Mirela sat down across from him. He swallowed. This was his chance. Before he could open his mouth, Ivy bounced to the table, flopped into the chair beside Mirela, and spread her napkin on her lap. She pointed to her plate. "They had cooked carrots. I love cooked carrots."

Josif nodded, trying to hold his frustration behind his tongue. They'd sit for another several minutes before his mom returned with her plate.

Ivy held out her hands and flipped them over. She looked at Mirela. "Did you wash your hands?"

Mirela nodded.

"I forgot." She placed the napkin on the table. "Be right back."

Josif cleared his throat. "It looked like you all were doing well at the bake sale."

"Yes." Mirela glanced at him for a moment then averted her gaze. "We seemed to do very well."

Bile rose in Joseph's mouth. He didn't recall being so nervous when he first asked Sabrina on a date. Then he remembered she'd asked him. He pushed thoughts of his ex-girlfriend out of his head. "Mirela, I was wondering. . ."

Mama arrived at the table and sat beside him. "Doesn't it

all look so good? I love this place." She looked around the room. "Where's Ivy? We need to say grace."

Ivy bounded to the table and sat beside Mirela. "I'm back."

"Good. Let's pray." Mama tapped his arm. "Will you, Josif?"

He nodded. *God, please get Ivy and Mama away from this table so that I can talk to Mirela.* He coughed, sure that Mama would not be pleased with his honest, unspoken petition to their Father. "Dear God, bless our food and our time together. Amen."

Mama peered at him. He knew the prayer was shorter, possibly a little less heartfelt than she expected, but he couldn't help it. Ants had taken up residence in his pants and he was anxious for the opportunity to get rid of them. But they weren't going anywhere until he was able to get Mirela alone.

Lunch was torture as the women, one by one, left the table for one food dish or another, but never, not once, did he get to sit at the table by himself with Mirela. He wanted to get some dessert, but he knew the moment he did Mirela would be left alone and he'd miss his chance.

I might as well just ask her in front of Mama and Ivy. I could even stand on a chair and announce it to the whole restaurant. It's the only way I'm going to get to do it.

He opened his mouth to just get it over with when Ivy stood and excused herself from the table. In the next instant, Mama stood and said she wanted some more ice cream. They were alone. Josif looked at Mirela. She didn't look at him but focused intently on the pie she was eating.

"Mirela."

She looked at him. Her brown eyes appeared vulnerable and innocent. Mirela wasn't a woman who played games.

She didn't flirt or manipulate. She was honest to herself and others, and he loved that about her.

He cleared his throat. He'd waited all through lunch for this moment, and his tongue felt as if it had swollen double its size. His mind seemed to have gone blank and he had no idea what words to say to her.

Do you want to go on a date? Do you want to go on a date? The words pounded through his head, but he couldn't seem to get them to form on his lips. "Mirela."

She furrowed her eyebrows. "Yes?"

He knew he was taking too long. He needed to just spit it out. Sweat beaded on the back of his neck, and his hands grew clammy. He was going to get sick. He was thirty years old, co-owner and manager of a successful hotel, and he was going to pass out from trying to ask a woman on a date.

This was ridiculous. He gripped his napkin in his hand and sat up straight in his chair. "Would you go to dinner with me?"

Mirela started to shake her head. "Josif, I—"

"Of course she would." Mama stood above Mirela's chair. She placed her hands on Mirela's shoulders. "Wouldn't you, dear? Of course you'll go out with Josif."

Mirela looked down at her plate. She'd been about to decline. But why? He'd fallen head over heels for her. Couldn't she feel it? They shared a connection. Surely he wasn't alone in his feelings.

Mama slid into Ivy's seat. "Friday night would probably be best for Josif. That would work for you, right?"

Mirela nodded, but she still hadn't looked back at Josif.

Mama continued. "You two can go see that new movie that's out. Matt took Sofija. It's about this guy who gets stuck in another city and he meets this girl." She peered at Josif.

"You were planning to take her to a movie, right?"

Josif pursed his lips and nodded. Ivy strode up to the table and furrowed her brows. Josif motioned for her to sit beside him. "Mama's planning a date."

"A date?"

"Mine and Mirela's."

"Oh." Ivy stared at Mama Sesely then Mirela.

Josif placed his elbow on the table and rested his cheek against his fist. He'd finally gotten up the nerve to ask her. She'd said yes, but it was obvious she didn't want to go. Mama continued to jabber on about the different restaurants where he could take her. He actually felt sorry for Mirela. Mama wasn't talking to him. Only her.

Now what am I supposed to do, God? Mama made sure I got the date with her.

He excused himself. Mama didn't notice anyway. He walked into the bathroom and stared at his reflection. Turning on the cold water, he splashed some in his face. Lunch hadn't gone as he hoped. It had been a complete disaster, and he had no idea how to fix it.

fifteen

Mirela groaned as she rummaged through her closet. She didn't know what she should wear for her date with Josif. She didn't want to be embarrassed to be in public, but she didn't want to look like she was trying to be attractive for him either. Flustered, she tightened the belt around her robe and flopped onto the bed. "Maybe I should just call and tell him I'm sick."

Ivy searched through Mirela's bottom dresser drawers. "Then Mama Sesely will set you up for next weekend."

Mirela covered her eyes with the back of her hand. "I don't know why she's so determined to have Josif and me go on a date. He has a girlfriend."

"Are you sure about that? Maybe they broke up."

Mirela sat up in her bed and crossed her legs. "I'm pretty sure. Less than one week ago I saw her arms all wrapped around him." She hugged herself then rubbed her shoulders. "Next she kissed him on the cheek." She blew a kiss into the air and then sprawled out on the bed again.

Ivy placed a hand on her hip and spoke in an overtly proper voice. "Mirela, I have never seen you behave so dramatically. I believe you've fallen for this young man."

Mirela rolled over. "What does it matter if I like him? He has a girlfriend."

"You know—"

"Don't you see?" Mirela tapped her forehead with her fingertips. "The man drives me crazy. He invades my head at all times of the day. And night. No matter how much I try to avoid him, he's there. But I need to stay away from him." Mirela frowned. "Know what makes this worse? I think the only reason he asked me out is because Mama Sesely is so set on us being together."

"You could have said no."

Mirela snorted. "Were you not at the restaurant with us? Did aliens come and momentarily snatch your body? There was no saying no to his offer."

A slight smile lifted Ivy's lips. She cocked her head. "I have to admit his mother is a bit persistent."

"Persistent!" Mirela flung open her arms. "She planned our date!"

Ivy bit her bottom lip, but Mirela could tell she was about to burst into giggles. The hilarity of the situation wafted over her, and Mirela found laughter bubbling up inside. Giving in to the emotion, she laughed with all that was in her. Ivy joined the revelry until tears streamed down both their cheeks.

Mirela patted her eyes with the belt of her robe while Ivy stood and wiped her face with the back of her hand. "We've got to find you an outfit. Something plain. Nothing too pretty."

"But I don't want to be embarrassed either."

Ivy wrinkled her nose. "Of course not." She tapped her index finger against her cheek. "You probably shouldn't wear makeup."

"Wasn't planning on it anyway."

"And I'll french braid your hair."

Mirela gasped. "I love it when my hair is braided. Are you saying it's ugly that way?"

"Not ugly. Plain."

Mirela humphed and crossed her arms in front of her

chest. "How could a bunch of knots in your hair look plain?"

Ivy smacked her hand against her leg. "Trust me. It does. Now let me french braid it."

Mirela stuck out her bottom lip. "Fine. But what should I wear?"

Ivy rummaged through the clothes. "This." She pulled out Mirela's favorite navy capris and a white polo shirt."

Mirela's mouth dropped open. "What's wrong with that outfit? I've worn it to work several times."

Ivy tossed the clothes on the bed beside Mirela. "Don't you get it? You don't want to look bad. We're fixing you up in something you'd wear to the day care, not on a date."

Mirela squinted her eyes at her sister. "It still kinda feels like you're belittling my regular attire."

Ivy pointed at the clothes. "Put those on, or I'm going to put them on you."

Mirela slipped into the outfit Ivy had selected, then sat in the chair while Ivy braided her hair. Mirela relaxed. Any anxiety she felt always seeped out of her when Ivy twined her fingers through her hair.

Once finished, Mirela stared at her reflection in the full-length mirror. "I look like I'm going to work."

"Exactly." Ivy clapped her hands then rubbed them together. "But you're not going to work. You're going on a date, so you should look a bit flashier than this."

Mirela frowned. "So this is me when I'm trying not to look attractive."

Ivy flicked Mirela in the arm.

Mirela squealed and rubbed the spot. "What are you doing?"

"I'm knocking some sense into you. You are not unattractive. Nothing I can do will make you unattractive. You just don't look like you're going on a hot date."

"I'm definitely not going on a hot date."

"I know."

"I'm going on a platonic date. He has a girlfriend. I am in no way interested in Josif Sesely."

Ivy rolled her eyes and swatted the air as she walked out of the room. "Now you're driving me crazy."

Mirela hollered after her. "I don't like Josif."

"Keep telling yourself that, sis."

Mirela peered at her reflection. She pointed her finger at herself. "You do not like Josif Sesely." She shook the finger at the mirror. "Do you hear me? You do not like. . ."

She slumped her shoulders then looked up at the ceiling. "I have officially lost it, Lord. I'm scolding myself in the mirror."

"Submit to Me, and I will make your paths straight."

The proverb slid through her mind like a cold glass of sweet tea on a hot summer's day. She had to trust God. She had to give herself, all of herself, to Him, and allow Him to guide her life. He would show her how to get through this date. It was obvious Josif felt a lot of pressure from his mom. Mirela did as well, but she had to trust that God would take care of it.

After slipping on her sandals, she walked to her mom's bedroom door and knocked. "It's almost time for Josif to pick me up."

"Have fun."

She could hear the tension in her mother's voice. She hadn't seen much of her mom the entire day. Mirela knew she was upset about the date, but she didn't know why. Her mother confused and baffled her every bit as much as her own feelings. *It's just one more reason why I'm going crazy.* The doorbell rang. *Perfect timing. Maybe I'll have a full meltdown before I make it to the door.*

Mirela sucked in a deep breath and walked toward her date. She opened the door, and Josif handed her a bouquet of pink and purple flowers.

She drank in the gift then looked up at him. "They're wonderful."

In her heart, she knew she wasn't only talking about the flowers. Josif looked incredibly handsome in a light green polo shirt and pressed khakis. His deep-brown eyes seemed to scream of adoration for her, and the scent of his woodsy cologne almost knocked her out of her sandals.

For a moment she wished she could run upstairs and change into something prettier. Something that would make her appear more feminine and appealing. She understood what Ivy had been trying to tell her. She didn't look bad, but she didn't look like a woman going on a date either.

She wished she'd left her hair down. Let it roll in waves down her shoulders. A bit of mascara and maybe a touch of lip gloss wouldn't have hurt. She'd have felt more comfortable. Maybe she could ask him to wait here for just a moment and she could run upstairs and do a quick makeover.

The vision of Sabrina's arms wrapped around Josif flashed through her mind. She wished she could get that picture out of her head. But it was a good reminder at the moment. She didn't need to daydream about fixing herself up for Josif.

This would be the one and only date she'd have with him. She needed to focus on that. Either he'd asked her out because his mother guilted him into it. Or he had wanted to ask her out despite his having a girlfriend. If the latter was the case, she wanted to get as far away from Josif Sesely as possible.

She pointed to the flowers. "Let me put these in a vase and we'll be on our way."

Josif nodded, and she realized he had yet to say a word to her. Again he acted as nervous as a dad waiting on his baby to make its first appearance in the world. But what possible reason did he have to act that way?

&

Josif salted his baked potato then placed the shaker back on the table. Mirela had excused herself from dinner for the second time, and she hadn't even had a bite to eat yet. She was acting weird. Really weird. He knew she'd agreed to the date because of Mama's persistence, but he'd hoped once it was just the two of them, the tension would lessen and they'd enjoy their time together.

"Sorry about that." Mirela slipped into the seat across from him.

"The food just arrived. It's still hot."

She nodded then lowered her gaze to her plate. She picked up her fork and knife and attacked the steak with unnecessary force. Although tempted to ask if she needed some assistance, he bit his tongue. He didn't want to offend her.

He took a bite of potato, swallowed, then dabbed his mouth with the napkin. "How was work today?"

Mirela looked up then averted her gaze. She pointed to the steer's head hanging on the wall. "Don't you think it's a little odd that they hang dead animals' heads on the walls? Does it really incite their patrons to want to eat the meat?"

Josif sat back, surprised by her questions. "I'm sorry. We didn't have to eat here. I thought you liked this steak house."

"Oh, I do." She jabbed a piece of steak in her mouth and chewed while she continued, "I just think it's weird."

Josif crinkled his nose. He'd never before had a date talk

and chew as if she were a cow chewing the cud. If it were Chloe eating that way he'd correct her.

She smacked her lips as she finished the bite then shoveled in a scoop of potato. Part of it fell from her lip and she didn't bother to wipe it. Something was definitely wrong. He'd eaten with Mirela on several occasions. She'd never displayed such bad manners.

"Mirela, is something the matter?"

She wiped her mouth and shook her head. "No. Of course not." She pointed to a family that had just been seated at the other side of the restaurant. "I used to watch their daughter. I should go say hi to them." She placed her napkin on the table. "I think I will."

He watched as she scooted out of the booth and headed toward the family. She hadn't even given him a chance to respond.

He took in her behavior with the family. Her bright smile lit up the room. The mother stood, obviously happy to see Mirela, and wrapped her in a big hug. He watched as they talked for several minutes. At one point it appeared the mother gestured for her to return to him, but she swatted the air and continued to talk.

Josif sighed. Not only was she exhibiting bad manners, but she was bordering on being downright rude. And what was up with her outfit. She was wearing a plain white shirt and a pair of short blue pants. It looked like she hadn't even changed since she left work.

He'd spent a full hour taking a long, hot shower, shaving to perfection, gelling his hair, and ironing his clothes. He'd inspected and reinspected himself, wanting to look his best for Mirela. He wondered if she may have some spot of baby vomit on her that he hadn't yet noticed.

After several minutes she returned to the table without so much as an apology and started eating again. He'd waited for her to return, and now his food was cold. Frustrated, he speared the steak he'd been looking forward to all day and shoved it in his mouth.

He stared at her until she finally met his gaze. "We don't have to go to a movie, you know."

A glimmer of something flashed across her expression. He could tell she knew she was being rude, and she felt bad for it. But why? Even if she felt bamboozled into the date from Mama, she could have called him and canceled. She didn't have to put on this little performance.

She placed her fork on the plate then put her hands in her lap. "I am feeling tired. It might be best if you take me on home."

There was a catch in her voice, like she was about to cry. She wasn't making any sense, and he was tired of playing games with her. He motioned for the waiter and requested their check.

After paying he followed her to the car, opened the door for her, and then moved around to the driver's side. The ride back to her house was a quiet one. He tried to focus on the street signs and lights. He considered turning on the radio, but he wasn't in the mood to hear anything.

He sneaked a peek at Mirela. She sat ramrod still, her gaze straight ahead. He'd fallen in love with her. Despite how she'd acted at the restaurant, despite her apparent dislike for him.

The scripture in Corinthians that spoke of love being patient and kind flitted through his mind. How it didn't envy or boast or keep record of wrongs. Love wasn't proud or easily angry or self-seeking. It protected. Trusted. Hoped. It persevered.

He pulled into her driveway, turned off the car, and opened his door. Mirela touched his hand, and Josif startled. He wanted to take her hand in his and feel the softness of it. He looked at her, but she was focused on her house. "You don't have to walk me to the door."

Her words felt like the detonation of the dynamite that crashed an old building, plunging it to the ground. She released his hand, and he watched as she walked up the sidewalk and then into the house. She didn't look back, not even to wave good-bye.

He rubbed his eyes and then his temples. Exhaustion from a long week was setting in. He peered up at the heavens. The sky was filled with stars. "God, I love her. After tonight, I don't know why. I don't know how it's happened so fast, but I know I do."

"Persevere."

The single word filled his mind and heart. Love always persevered, and with Mirela he'd have to wait. He'd have to give her time and space and wait. "God, I've never felt so sure of my feelings, such peace with Your will. Now, give me the patience to wait for her."

He started the car and pulled out of the driveway with a sense of peace he hadn't expected. Paul's words echoed through his mind. *God's strength is most powerful when I am weak.*

sixteen

The last thing Mirela wanted to do was drive to Gatlinburg after church. It had been only two days since her date with Josif. Heat still warmed her cheeks each time she thought of how poorly she'd acted. She should have just come out and asked Josif why he would ask her out when he was dating Sabrina. There was a reason God's Word said the truth shall set you free. The games she'd played Friday night had held her captive in embarrassment.

She didn't know how she would respond if she saw Josif. *I need to have a backbone and just fess up. He's the one trying to go out with two women.* Appeasing his mother or not, she should have just called him out on it.

After parking the car, she pulled down the visor and checked her teeth for any remnants of the crunchy taco she'd practically swallowed whole on the drive over. She pulled a stick of gum out of her purse and popped it into her mouth.

She closed her eyes as her heart began to race. *Just calm down. The likelihood of seeing Josif is slim. He's off on Sundays. He probably won't be here.*

Taking a deep breath, she stepped out of the car and pressed the wrinkles from her dark gray A-line skirt. The weather had gotten cooler. A slight breeze blew and she gripped the sides of her sweater, holding them to her chest. Determined to walk straight to Mama Sesely's apartment, she barreled into the building.

Someone grabbed her arm and she turned and saw Sabrina.

Dressed in her rhinestone dotted shirt, the woman sparkled brighter than the sun. Her jeans hugged every curve of her legs, all the way to the top of her high-heeled black boots. Her hair, her makeup, everything about Sabrina screamed movie-star perfection.

Mirela's heart sank. She was no competition for the woman, even if she wanted to be. *Which I don't.* She blew out a quick breath. Mirela hoped Sabrina hadn't heard about their ridiculous date and was now planning to confront her. Sabrina smiled. "I have got to tell you about the amazing date I had last night."

Mirela furrowed her brows. She didn't want to hear about Sabrina and Josif. She wanted to pick up the batteries and flashlights for the shoeboxes. Mama Sesely had told her she didn't have room to store them.

Sabrina lifted up her pointer finger. Mirela noted that even her long, red fingernails had diamond rhinestones on them. "First, he picked me up and took me to a snazzy restaurant. The seafood was absolutely divine. Have you had lobster bisque?"

Mirela shook her head, and Sabrina touched her hand to her neck. She looked up at the ceiling. "It is absolutely divine."

She looked back at Mirela then grabbed her arm with both hands. Mirela tried to nonchalantly pull away, but Sabrina's grip was too tight. "After that we went to a piano bar, and he paid the pianist to play a song just for me. Our song, of course."

Mirela frowned. Piano bar? That didn't sound like Josif at all. At least not the Josif she knew. But what did she know of the man? Subconsciously she'd studied his mannerisms. She could tell when he was frustrated or nervous. But she didn't really know Josif. Maybe he frequented piano bars all the time.

Sabrina continued. "Then he took me by the hand and guided me to the front of the bar and danced with me." She placed her hands against her stomach. "I can still feel the butterflies. It was like he and I were the only two people in the room. I mean—"

Mirela lifted her hand to stop Sabrina from torturing her any further. "I'm sorry, Sabrina. I'm really in a hurry. I need to get some items from Mama Sesely then be on my way." She started to walk away when her manners kicked in. She turned back around and forced a smile to her lips. "It was nice talking to you. Have a good day."

A smile that could only be explained as sinister lifted the woman's lips. She offered a brief nod, and Mirela turned back around. She could not believe Josif would take Sabrina out the very day after he'd taken her on a date. The gall of the man. She stomped to the older couples' apartment door and knocked harder than she'd intended.

Mama opened it and wrapped her in a bear hug. Mirela tried to keep her emotions in check as she visited with the couple for a few minutes. She looked at her watch. "I'm sorry, but I won't be able to stay today." She tapped her lips with her finger. "I do need to run by Josif's house. . . . He is at home, don't you suppose?"

"Actually he's in the office. He had a busy day yesterday and didn't get all the paperwork done."

I just bet he had a busy day. Taking out two women in one weekend would make anyone get backed up on his work. She smiled at Mama Sesely and pointed to the boxes. "I'll just come back and get those after I speak with Josif."

The older woman patted Mirela's knee. "Was your date with Josif fun?"

A moment of sadness washed through her as she wished she could tell Mama what a scoundrel her son was. Instead she stood and said, "It was interesting. Enlightening. But I'll be right back."

Mirela walked out of the apartment and stomped toward the office. The man was despicable, contemptible, reprehensible, and more. He'd played Sabrina and her, even his own mother. He claimed to be a Christian, but a Christian would never behave as he had. She pounded the door then yanked it open before he had the chance to respond.

Josif dropped his stack of papers onto the desk and stood. "Mirela. I didn't expect to see you—"

Mirela glared at him. "How—how could you?"

Josif's eyebrows drew together in a straight line as he frowned. "How could I what?"

She lifted her hands in the air. "Why would you ask me out? You have a girlfriend. What kind of man are you?" She pointed to her chest. "I know you were raised better than that. I know your parents."

"Mirela, what are you—"

"You took me out Friday night then Sabrina on Saturday." She opened her arms wide. "To a piano bar?" She scrunched up her face. "Really? I know I haven't known you long, but I just can't see you—"

"Mirela, I have no idea—"

She crossed her arms in front of her chest. "Oh really. Really? You have no idea." She opened her arms wide again. "Josif, you're supposed to be a Christian. You don't ask a woman on a date when you have a girlfriend." She lifted up three fingers. "A girlfriend you've had for three years."

"Mirela, I don't have a girlfriend."

&

"What?"

Josif walked around the desk and grabbed her arms. "I don't have a girlfriend."

She pulled away. "Yes you do. You and Sabrina have been

dating for three years."

He shook his head. "We broke up over a month ago. While you were on vacation with your family. I told Papa. I just assumed he told Mama and she told you."

Mirela frowned and lowered herself into a chair. She shook her head. "No. That's not right. I saw the two of you hugging in the courtyard just last week. She kissed your cheek."

Josif scratched his jaw. He tried to remember when he'd talked to Sabrina in the courtyard. His memory clicked. It was the day he was checking on Mama's flower selection. He remembered he thought Sabrina acted funny when she came outside to talk with him. Surely she hadn't seen Mirela and then purposely tried to make her jealous. And yet Sabrina wasn't the woman Josif thought she was.

He leaned against the top of the desk. "She was telling me about her date. I don't know why she gave me a hug or kissed my cheek, but I can assure you I was not expecting it, and I did not reciprocate."

"But. . ." She placed her fingertips against her temples and rubbed. "You took her to a snazzy restaurant and a piano bar yesterday, and you—"

Josif touched his chest. "She said I took her out yesterday?"

Mirela's expression pinched up as if she'd just eaten a sour lemon. "Well, she didn't say your name. She said he, but you two are dating."

He couldn't resist. He reached out to touch a length of her hair. Today it flowed in long waves down the right side of her shoulder. It was every bit as soft as he imagined. "I am not dating Sabrina."

"But Mama Sesely said you had a busy day yesterday, and—"

He took Mirela's hand in his and helped her to her feet.

She stood mere inches away. He only needed to dip his head, and he could feel her lips against his. "I was at my nephews' football games."

He brushed a strand of hair away from her face and tucked it behind her ear. Her gaze seemed to search his for honesty. The intensity of it drew him closer, and he feared he'd release more honesty than she was ready for. Forcing himself to tear his gaze from hers, he pressed his lips against her forehead and whispered, "I'm not dating anyone." *But you're the one I want to date. Forever.*

A sigh escaped her lips as she wrapped her arms around his waist and buried her face in his shirt. He tucked her into his embrace, relishing the scent of her hair and the softness of her touch. Her back heaved and his heart grew heavy, knowing her tears would soon be dampening his shirt. A muffled sound came from her lips. He patted her back and allowed his fingers to rake the length of her hair.

The sound grew louder, and he realized she wasn't crying. As Josif pushed her away from his embrace, she laughed. Her hysterics grew until she doubled over, snorted, then flopped herself back into the chair.

Josif stared at her. Unease snaked its way through him. Why was she laughing? He tried to grin at her, to figure a way to join her revelry, but he couldn't decipher what was so funny. She'd thought him to be a two-timer, to be unfaithful in his commitment to God.

She smacked her hands against the arm of the chair. "You're kidding, right?"

Josif crossed his legs and leaned against the desk, then gripped the top with both hands. Irritation welled within him. "I would not make a joke about something so important."

She slapped her hand against her head. "I am such a

goober. I always do this." She smacked her hand against the arm of the chair. "I'm known for it. I jump to conclusions before I know all the facts." She twisted in her chair. "You'd think I'd have learned by now. As many times as truth has socked me in the face."

Josif grinned. The Mirela he'd talked with at the Chinese restaurant was back. The one he'd fallen in love with. "It sounds like Sabrina had a little bit to do with keeping you confused."

Mirela crossed her legs as she shook her head. "No. I can't blame my confusion on someone else. I should have just come right out and asked you." She clasped her hands. "It's just that whenever I'm around you. . ."

Josif grabbed her hand and helped her up. "Come here." He guided her to the courtyard, praying that no one would be there and that God would direct his words. They'd spent enough time chasing confusion. He wanted to be upfront with her.

Once outside, he breathed a silent prayer of thanks for the solitude of the green area. He motioned for her to sit on a bench then sat beside her. "I want to tell you something."

Her breathing was labored, and he imagined her thoughts were whirling with the possibilities of what he planned to share. Perhaps she was already jumping to conclusions again. He bit back a grin. "Remember when Mama said you were my future wife?"

Her cheeks blushed as she averted his gaze and nodded.

"Well, there's a story with that."

She looked back at him. Her eyes seemed to beg him to go on.

"Apparently when you were born, I was quite enamored with you. I guess I couldn't keep my hands off your head, your hands. I was always wanting to hold you." *Not much has changed, has it, Lord? I still want to touch her face, hold her hands, and I'm dying for the opportunity to wrap my arms around her again.*

Mirela giggled, and for a moment he feared she'd heard his unspoken prayer. Knowing she couldn't have, he continued, "I guess it was at that time that our mothers decided that one day we would be together." He stared into her eyes, searching for her inward response. "As husband and wife."

She gasped. "I knew you asked me out because your mother wanted it, but please do not think that just because our mothers planned—"

Josif placed his hand on hers. "No. Let me finish."

She snapped her mouth shut then chewed on the inside of her lip.

"I couldn't believe it when Mama told me that she saw your picture in the newspaper, realized it was you, and that was how she presented it to me." He chuckled and pointed to his palm, pretending it was the article. He mimicked his mother's voice, "Josif, here is your future wife."

Mirela's cheeks brightened again as she looked up at the sky. "I can't believe—"

He stopped her. "I thought she was crazy. I'd been dating Sabrina for three years. I was comfortable with her. Hotel renovations were complete. We were finally getting the business we'd worked so hard for. I was working more regular hours. It was time to think about settling down. With Sabrina. Then you came along."

He stood and then paced in front of her.

"Josif, please—"

He lifted his hand. "Anyway, because of you I saw my family through fresh eyes. I began to realize all I'd missed.

I'd become too work driven, too self-absorbed, and I'd lost the intimacy of my relationship with God. He drew me back to Himself, and I realized Sabrina wasn't the one for me. But you. . ."

Mirela stood. "Josif, just because our mothers—"

"Don't you see? I don't want to date you because of our mothers. Your spirit intrigues me. Uplifts me. When I see you with Mama and my sister, I. . ." He brushed the same strand of wayward hair away from her face. "And your hair absolutely mesmerizes me."

She bit her bottom lip. He knew she was attracted to him. He could see it in her eyes. Everything in him wanted to lower his head and claim her lips. But it wasn't time. Not yet.

He moved his hand away from her face. "Mirela, I want you to go on a date with me. Not because of our mothers, and knowing that I don't have a girlfriend. I want you to go on a date with me because you want to. Will you?"

Josif held his breath as Mirela studied him. He had no idea what thoughts tracked through her mind. Usually they were never what he expected them to be anyway. After what seemed years, she nodded. "Yes."

seventeen

As she drove home, Mirela passed Cheryl on the street. She waved and her colleague's face lit up as she waved back. Mirela parked and walked into her house. Spying Ivy, she motioned behind her with her thumb. "Was Cheryl here?"

Ivy lifted her shoulders and smiled. "She was. She was having a bad day and 'something'"—Ivy winked while using her fingers to draw quotations marks in the air— "made her want to stop by our house. I'd say that was God working on her heart."

Mirela smiled. "Sounds like it."

"Well, I invited her in, got her some tea, listened to her talk about Kyle for a while, then I invited her to join our Bible study."

"What did she say?"

"Said she couldn't wait."

Mirela's mouth fell open. "You're kidding?"

Ivy shrugged again. "God's always working, sis."

"That's the truth."

Ivy squinted at Mirela. "There's seems to be a bit more meaning behind that statement." She snapped her fingers. "Spill it."

Mirela chuckled. She had every intention of sharing her and Josif's discussion with Ivy. Again her heart filled with thanksgiving for her sister. Ivy had been a constant blessing since Mirela's adoption. Not only a good friend, Ivy was also an honest accountability partner—even when Mirela didn't *want* to be held accountable. She opened her arms wide. "Josif isn't dating Sabrina."

"I knew it. He loves you, doesn't he?"

Mirela's heart sped up. "He didn't say that."

"But he does."

"Ivy."

Her sister grabbed her hand and pulled her down onto the couch. "I want all the juicy details. Everything."

Mirela told her about their talk and about her confusion about Sabrina. She even shared about what their mothers had decided when Mirela was just a baby. Ivy's eyes widened with each revelation.

Ivy finally placed her hand on her chest and said, "God truly does have His hand in everything. Absolutely everything. Only God could reunite you and Josif." She touched Mirela's hand. "What colors are you going to pick for the wedding? You love blue, and it's a good color on me since I'll be your maid of honor."

Mirela laughed. "Don't you think it's a little early to be planning a wedding?"

"I certainly do."

Mirela turned at the sound of her mom's voice. With arms crossed in front of her chest, her mother tapped her right foot against the floor. It reminded Mirela of the time she and Ivy had been horsing around in the living room and broke her mom's vase. But they weren't little kids anymore, and her mother's frustration with her didn't make sense.

Her mom started to walk to her bedroom. Mirela jumped up and touched her mom's elbow. "Don't leave. You keep locking yourself up in your room. I don't know why you're upset."

Ivy raced around to the front of their mom. "Mirela's right.

Tell us"—she pointed to Mirela—"or at least tell her why you're so upset. I just don't believe it's because you're jealous of Mirela's biological mother."

Her mother wrinkled her face. "Oh my, no." She looked at Mirela. "Maybe a little, but I'm glad Mrs. Sesely gave you that picture. It's good to have some memory of your mother."

Mirela hugged her mom. "You're the only mom I've ever known. I love you."

Her mother returned the embrace. "Honey, I know that."

They stood still for a moment, and Mirela realized her shoulder was getting wet from her mother's silent tears. Mirela pulled away and searched her expression. "There's something else. What is it?"

Her mom exhaled a deep breath, walked to the rocking chair, and then sat down. Her lower lip quivered. "I'm afraid you'll leave me."

Ivy moved around to the couch and sat across from her. "Mom, don't you want us to get married and have a family? You've always—"

Her mother lifted her hands. "Of course, I pray both you girls will have a relationship like the one I had with your daddy."

Mirela found her voice. "But it's more than that, isn't it?"

Her mother started rocking. "You've always had such a heart for missions. Especially the people of Serbia. Just like your dad."

"Mom, she's Serbian." Ivy pointed back at Mirela. "Of course she's going to have a heart for her own people."

Her mother speared Ivy with a glare. "I know that, Ivy." She looked back at Mirela. "It's just that. . ." She rocked more fervently and shook her head. "My feelings are so wrong. God's been dealing with me, and I'm trying to give them over to Him. To trust Him. But it's hard."

Mirela stood plastered to her spot on the floor. It seemed to be a day of confessions no matter where she turned. "Mom, I don't understand."

"It was hard for me to minister in Serbia. I went. I prayed daily for God's peace and strength, and He provided. But I longed for the States. In my heart, I was glad when we had to return."

"But what does that have to do with Josif and his family?"

"I've already lost your father. I don't think I can stand to lose either of you. I'm afraid he'll take you back to Serbia. To live."

Ivy's voice was quiet, just above a whisper. "Who, Mom? Josif? Or God?"

Tears rolled down her mother's face and she reached over and took Ivy's chin in her hand. "My sweet child, God has given you such a wonderful gift of discernment. In my head, I know it would be God and not the Sesely family who would take her back to Serbia, but in my heart. . ." She made a fist and tapped her chest.

Finally able to move, Mirela walked to her mother and placed a hand on her shoulder. "For the record, I don't feel called to move to Serbia, and I believe the Sesely family is pretty settled in Gatlinburg, but if God asked—"

Her mom patted her hand. "Honey, I know, and I would never want you to go against God's will. His ways are always best."

Her mom stood and wrapped her arms around Mirela. Ivy hopped up and joined the hug. Once separated, her mom wiped her eyes with the back of her hand. Ivy grabbed a tissue from the table and handed it to her.

Her mom gave Mirela a half smile. "For the record, Josif

seems like a nice young man, and his family is wonderful."

Mirela grinned. "Thanks, Mom."

&

Josif had gone back to his office to finish up the paperwork, but he couldn't focus. He had another date with Mirela. He believed he'd enjoy this one. To think she'd thought he was still dating Sabrina. *Papa tells Mama everything. I just assumed. . .* He smacked his thigh. *That's what I get for assuming.*

He remembered the mischievous smile on Sabrina's lips when she'd hugged him that day in the courtyard. He'd been blind to her true nature. Her manipulation went deeper than simply wanting him or Mirela to be jealous. Hers was a faith problem. *God, I should have been a better witness. I shouldn't have been so blind.*

He stood and walked down the hall. He'd beaten himself up enough about his actions over the last three years. He knew God had forgiven him, and the constant reminders and feelings of guilt about it were not from the Lord.

Needing to pick up his ironed dress shirts and slacks, he strode to his parents' apartment. In a way, it was pathetic that his mother still ironed his clothes. But truthfully it was just easier that way. He'd had to fight his mother to let him do his own laundry. She'd insisted there was no reason she couldn't do it for him. Winning battles with Mama was no easy task. He'd finally gotten her to agree to let him do his own laundry as long as she could do the ironing. He hated ironing, and who was he to argue anyway?

He opened the apartment door and called, "Hello, Mama, Papa. I've come to get my clothes."

Mama walked into the living area. She pointed to the closet. "They're finished and in there. Your papa is at Sofija's."

She pulled him over to the couch and practically pushed him to sit down. "I saw you talking to Mirela in the courtyard. I will get some cookies and you tell me all about it."

Josif tried to sit up but she stood above him. "No cookies, Mama."

"Does Sabrina know about Mirela?"

"Sabrina and I broke up."

Mama placed her hand against her chest and looked up at the ceiling. "Praise God."

"Mama, that's not very nice."

She placed her hand on his. "I pray for Sabrina, Josif. I do, but she is not right for you. She is bitter and—"

Josif lifted his hand to stop her. It hurt that he'd been so blind. "I know, and I'm praying for her, too."

"Do you have another date with Mirela?"

"Mama."

She smacked her hand against her hip. "I'm not getting any younger, Josif. I want as many years as possible to play with my grandchildren."

"I don't believe you're going to die soon, Mama. You're only in your fifties."

She grinned as she lifted her pointer finger. "Late fifties."

He wanted to add that she was too stubborn and opinionated to pass away. She was determined to rule his life for many years to come. But he held his tongue.

With a sigh, he nodded. "Yes, Mama. We have another date."

She clapped her hands. "Good. I have something to give you."

Josif groaned. There was no telling what the woman scampered off to collect. She had the best of intentions but he had to get her to understand that she was not in charge of his life. That job had been taken from the rightful person for too long, and now he was determined to allow God to run his life.

His mother returned with a small black box in her hand. She sat on the couch beside him and pressed it into his hand. "Open it."

He looked inside and saw a perfect, circular green opal. The stone was probably a centimeter big, and he knew it was one that had come from the mountains in Serbia. He gazed at his mother. "What is this for?"

"I've saved it all these years for you to have set into a piece of jewelry for your wife. She will carry a piece of your heritage." She lifted her eyebrows. "And possibly hers."

Josif snapped the box shut. "Mama, you must stop this matchmaking with Mirela. If God has chosen her as my wife, then she will be my wife. But you must not get in the way. Mirela and I can fall in love with each other without your assistance."

"Oh, I know this." His mother folded her hands in her lap. "You have already fallen in love, and I am not the one who caused it."

There was no reasoning with the woman. "Mama—"

"Take the stone, Josif. Decide to make it into what you will." She stood. "I've got to get supper started. I want you to give the opal to your wife." She winked. "Whoever she may be."

After Mama left the room, he leaned forward, placed his elbow on the coffee table, then smacked his forehead into his hand. He'd have to marry Mirela simply because no other woman would stand a chance surviving his mother.

He sat up and opened the box again. The light green opal reminded him of the mountains of his homeland, and how green the grass and trees looked in spring. Mirela would love this opal. She'd treasure that it had come from her native land.

An idea took shape in his mind. He knew what he would do with the stone, and he knew when he would give it to her—in less than a month. *God, maybe I need to slow down in my thinking.*

But his spirit felt such peace. It was right, and he knew it. He picked up a piece of scratch paper off the notepad Mama kept on the coffee table for the grandkids. He drew a square setting that would encase the green opal. Two diamonds would adorn each side. It would have to be yellow gold, as it looked beautiful against the light color of the stone.

He folded the paper and placed it inside his wallet. Mirela would love it. He'd need to take it to a jeweler first thing in the morning, as he wasn't sure how long it would take to fashion the jewelry. *Hopefully it will be ready in time.*

He grabbed his clothes out of the closet and yelled goodbye to his mom. After shutting the door, he walked down the hall. *It seems awful quick, Lord.*

His spirit remained at peace, and he knew when it was right it was right. Besides, hadn't his mother been praying for them for years?

eighteen

Mirela slipped the knee-length black dress over her head. It hugged her trim stomach and then flared at the bottom. She felt like Marilyn Monroe in *The Seven Year Itch*, only Mirela's dress wasn't white, and it wasn't low cut on top, and she wasn't standing over an air vent on the street.

She twirled around in front of the mirror, allowing the skirt to fly through the air. She felt cute. She looked cute. She hoped Josif would think so, too.

The doorbell rang, and she raced toward it. She was thankful her mom was working second shift and Ivy had gone out with friends. She didn't want any silly comments from her sister or scowls from her mother, although her mother's attitude had softened considerably since they'd talked. It felt as if it had taken a lifetime to go on her first real date with Josif, and she wanted it to be perfect.

She still thought him silly to insist he pick her up for their date. They were going to a nice restaurant in Gatlinburg, then to the Titanic Museum. She'd never been to the museum and had wanted to go for some time. He had to drive all the way from Gatlinburg to Greenfield, then back to Gatlinburg for the date, then back to Greenfield to take her home, then back to Gatlinburg to go to his house. He'd travel a total of three hours just to go on a date with her. Thrills raced down her spine. But it made her feel special that he would do such a thing.

Sucking in a deep breath, she smiled as she opened the

door. Her heart fell. It was Emily. With Benny. And he was crying.

"Mirela, I am so sorry. I've been trying to call you. They called me in to work. I found someone to take Bella, but—" Emily looked at the baby then back at her—"I don't know what else to do."

Something was wrong. Emily worked in an office. She'd have no reason to work at night. Especially a Saturday night. She peered into the driveway and saw a man sitting in the driver's seat of Emily's car. Mirela looked at Emily. "I'm sorry. I have a date."

"Please," Emily begged.

Mirela battled her inward confront-or-not-to-confront war. She looked at Emily's car again. Something didn't feel right. Her parents had always taught her to trust her spirit.

Flustered, Emily turned. "Forget it. I'll take him with me."

Mirela touched Emily's arm. She'd never forgive herself if something happened to Benny. She reached for the baby. "Give him to me."

Without another word, Emily handed him to her. She draped the diaper bag on Mirela's free shoulder and waved as she skipped to jump in the car beside the man Mirela had never seen before. Mirela's heart ached for Bella and Benny. Emily had worked so hard, but lately something had changed, and she'd pawned the children off on anyone who was willing to take them.

She walked back into the house. Rubbing noses with Benny, she said, "We'll just have to keep praying for Mommy, won't we?"

Benny smiled, then his body jerked and he vomited all down the front of her dress. She gasped as she held him away from her body. In three years of day-care work, she'd never seen so much puke.

Nearing tears, she used pillows to sit the seven-month-old up on the floor. Rushing into the kitchen, she patted the mess off her dress and then dabbed a rag in water and soap and tried to get out the smell. By the time she finished, her dress was two shades of black and she couldn't tell if she still smelled like upchuck. The scent seemed to have cemented itself to her nostrils.

The doorbell rang again. This time she knew it was Josif. She shuffled to the front door and opened it. The smile on his face faded as he looked her up and down. He handed her a beautiful bouquet of pink roses, then pointed at the side of her face. "You got a little something in your hair."

Mirela growled and raced into the bathroom. She wiped the vomit out of her hair, then trudged back into the living room. Josif sat on the couch, staring at Benny.

She wrinkled her nose. "I've got Benny."

"I can see that." He looked at her. She wondered what he thought of her. Only thirty minutes ago, she'd believed she looked pretty. Now she looked like the mother of a seven-month-old. Only she didn't have the privilege of him actually being her child.

"It wasn't expected."

"I assumed as much."

She swung her arm. "Do you want to reschedule?"

Josif smiled. "Let's just take him with us."

Mirela blushed with a mixture of shyness and pleasure. "Okay."

Josif stood and walked toward her. Her heart sped up as he cupped her chin in his hand. "I've been looking forward to seeing you all day."

Certain that her cheeks were still tinted pink, Mirela

shifted her gaze to her feet then back up at him. "Me, too."

"One thing." He plugged his nose with his thumb and index finger. "You may want to change out of that dress."

Mirela's jaw dropped as she saw the merriment that lit his eyes. She swatted at his arm. "Josif!" She lifted part of the fabric to her nose and winced. "I think you're right. Give me five minutes."

&

Josif looked at Mirela across the table. Though her orange sweater and straight brown skirt were not as fancy as the black dress, Mirela still looked beautiful. He glanced at the baby sitting in the highchair that fit under the table. Slobber ran down his chin as Benny blew bubbles and patted the table with his chubby hand.

The date was not going as Josif expected, but he didn't mind. Mirela was eating dinner with him because she wanted to, not because his mother had coerced her into it.

"Well, what a surprise."

Josif glanced to the side and saw Sabrina and a blond-haired man standing beside their table. Anger raced through his veins as he fought the urge to tell Sabrina off after she'd led Mirela to believe they were still dating.

"Hi, Sabrina." Mirela's voice was cool and kind, and when Josif looked at her he didn't detect any frustration.

Sabrina lifted her eyebrows. "Having kids already?"

"He's obviously not ours." Josif spit the words through gritted teeth.

Mirela smiled. "No. This is one of the babies I take care of." She grabbed Benny's hand and waved it. "He just wanted to come to dinner with us. Didn't you, Benny?"

Disdain wrapped Sabrina's face as she seemed to realize her quips weren't upsetting Mirela. "Still, I'm surprised to see you." Sarcasm dripped from her lips and she glared at Josif.

He pursed his lips together, determined not to say another word. If he did he'd spend most of the night asking God's forgiveness for the sharp edge of his tongue.

"It was really good to see you, Sabrina." Mirela's voice was soft and sincere. "Enjoy your dinner."

Sabrina huffed as she turned and guided her date to their table. Josif studied Mirela. He could tell that seeing Sabrina hurt her, but she didn't say anything. She didn't cut on her dress or the shoes she wore. She didn't belabor the many offenses Sabrina had committed against her. She didn't say anything.

Their food arrived, and Josif took Mirela's hands in his to pray. "God, bless this food and our date tonight. Thank You for Mirela. She is such a wonderful, beautiful woman. Amen."

Mirela looked up at him and smiled. "You forgot to thank God for you."

He laughed. "That's your job."

She saluted him. "Got it."

He took a bite of his chicken cordon bleu. It practically melted in his mouth. He nodded to her parmesan-crusted steak. "Good?"

She nodded. "Delicious. I could eat steak every day."

Benny jabbered and patted the table through their meal and then contentedly ate his baby food. Afraid the little guy wouldn't make it through the museum, Mirela suggested he take her home.

They walked to the car, and Mirela fastened Benny in his car seat then slipped into the front beside him. She locked her seat belt and looked up at Josif.

He lifted his hand and gently touched her cheek with his

palm. "I'm sorry you didn't get to see the museum. I know you wanted to go."

He watched her swallow and wondered if she longed for his touch as much as he'd yearned to feel the softness of her cheek. She smiled. "It's okay."

He started the car and pulled out of the parking lot and onto the road. Benny started to fuss, so Mirela unbuckled her seat belt and turned around to fix Benny's pacifier. She pressed against him, her head just inches from his. He wanted to tilt his head just a bit and kiss her, but then he would probably wreck the car and injure them all. *I don't want to do that, Lord.*

Mirela shifted back to face the front then snapped on her seat belt. "I'm glad we got to go to dinner." She placed her hand on his, sending shivers up and down it. "I'm just glad Benny was good."

"Me, too. So when are we going to go out again?"

She chuckled. "You sure you want to risk another date? You know I sometimes come with extras."

Josif grabbed her hand and squeezed it, but he didn't let go. He waited to see if she would pull it back. She didn't. "I don't mind the extras."

All too quickly he pulled into her driveway, got out, and pulled Benny in his car seat out of the back. She hefted her purse and the diaper bag on her shoulder. The sleeping baby didn't move as Josif hefted him and his car seat up the walk.

Mirela searched her purse for the front door key. After several moments, Josif said, "You know they say a woman will lose her keys when she's wanting a kiss good night."

Mirela gazed up at him. Her eyes sparkled with mischief. She raised one eyebrow. "Do they?"

Excitement swirled in his gut, and he placed Benny and

his car seat on the ground. He gently touched her forearms as he peered into her eyes. "Would you like a kiss tonight?"

She shrugged and bit her bottom lip. "Maybe."

He pulled her to him and pressed her lips to his. Desire welled within him. He hadn't meant to claim her with such force, but he'd thought of her lips and the softness of her skin until he nearly ached with the need to kiss her.

He lifted his head, but Mirela raked her fingers through his hair and pulled his lips back to her own. He pushed away. He had to, or he'd never be able to let her go.

He took a deep breath and looked into her eyes. They seemed to beg him to kiss her again. He touched her cheek with the back of his hand. "Mirela."

She lifted her chin, and he couldn't help himself. He kissed her one last time. Quick. Then he stepped away from her. He jingled the keys in his hands. "I've got to go. I can't wait to see you again."

She waved at him. When he got in the car, he saw that she touched her lips with her fingertips. He thought he would explode if she didn't hurry and get in the house. It took every ounce of resolve he had not to race back up that walk and wrap her in his arms again.

She lifted her keys out of her purse and unlocked the door and then waved to Josif one last time before carrying Benny inside. Josif blew out a slow breath as he waved back. *God, I don't think we'll be able to have a long engagement. I want that woman as my wife.*

nineteen

Mirela could hardly believe it was the last day to fill shoe-boxes for the year. She looked around the church's fellowship hall at the masses of shoeboxes and items that would be neatly tucked into them. Even more amazing was the amount of people who'd joined them in the outreach. She'd never seen so many volunteers ready to give hope to a child in another country. God had used the newspaper article to draw people to the ministry. Many helpers didn't even attend their small church.

God had also used the article to bring Josif to her. She peeked at the man who sat beside her. He seemed to be listening intently to what her pastor said from the portable podium, as should she. Especially since he would call her to the front to share her testimony in a matter of minutes. Still, she couldn't help taking a moment to thank God for Josif.

They'd spent almost every evening together the past few weeks. She knew it was quick, but she loved him. It seemed God had fashioned him just for her, and her for him.

Josif looked at her and grinned. She'd been caught staring at him. He nudged her leg. "He called for you."

Heat washed through her, and she knew her neck and cheeks blazed red as she walked to the microphone. There had to be at least fifty people packed into their small fellowship hall. She'd never spoken in front of so many people before, and she felt her hands tremble. *Lord, give me strength.*

"Just tell them what you know." The words her dad had often said to her and Ivy when they were small girls washed over her. He'd assured them they could share their faith with anyone at any time. All they needed to do was tell others what God had done for them personally in their lives.

She cleared her throat and looked up at the ceiling. "When I was little, I lived in Serbia. My parents died when I was a toddler, and my sister and her husband took care of me."

Her memories of Serbia were limited, but at that moment she remembered chasing her older sister on a dirt road when she'd gone to collect water. Her cousins had stayed back at their hovel, but Mirela hadn't. A deep memory of fear surfaced. She'd been afraid her sister would be taken from her just like her parents.

Love for the children who would receive the boxes overwhelmed her, and she looked at the faces in the crowd. They needed to know, needed to understand how important these simple gifts were to the children who received them.

"When I was five, two men and a woman brought a big truck to our town. I remember them jumping out of the cab, racing around to the back, and opening it. They started passing out shoeboxes."

Feeling tears well in her eyes, she swiped them away with the back of her hand. "At first I didn't know what the boxes were. Until I saw one of my cousins open his. It was filled with toys and candy. Things I'd never seen before."

"Then Carol, that was the woman's name, handed me a shoebox. I opened it and there sat my doll. I named her Carol after the woman. It was my very first doll." She lifted her shoulders and smiled. "I admit she still sits on my bed to this day."

The people laughed, and Mirela noted a few of the women

had tears pooling in their eyes. Mama and Papa Sesely, who would have driven themselves to help with the shoeboxes if Josif hadn't brought them, held each other's hands as they wiped their eyes and noses with tissues.

"But the presents weren't the best part." She chuckled. "Although they were pretty important to me at age five. The best part was when the men and Carol started reading to us about Jesus. I've learned that my mama and papa were Christians. But it was my sister and her husband, nonbelievers, who were raising me, so I didn't know about our Savior."

She opened her hands like they were a book. "But then Carol started reading about a man who loved me so much that He died for me. Even though I did bad things. He died for me. I remember thinking that day about how I'd pushed my baby cousin down because she'd made me mad, and I knew that I was bad."

She pointed to her chest. "I asked Jesus into my heart that day." She reached for an empty shoebox and then held it up. "It all started from this simple gift."

Her heart yearned to say more, to beg them to understand how God had used this ministry to reach her and so many like her. But her hands trembled and her knees felt weak. The Spirit quickened her. She'd said all that was necessary. Now it was time to work.

She walked back to her seat beside Josif. When she sat, he wrapped his arm around her shoulder and squeezed. Josif was a wonderful man. God was her ultimate strength, but He'd given her Josif and his strength as well. She pressed herself closer to him while the pastor prayed for the helpers and the work they would do that night.

She kept her eyes closed for a moment longer after the

pastor finished. *God, bless these shoeboxes. Every one of them. May the children who receive them come to know You as their personal Lord and Savior.*

She opened her eyes and was wrapped into Mama and Papa Sesely's arms. Mama kept repeating, "God is so good."

Once they released her, Mirela's mom walked up to her and folded her arm around Mirela's. "You did a good job."

She looked at her hands. "My hands were trembling."

Her mom kissed her cheek. "But your heart spoke loud and clear. I'm so proud of you."

Mirela felt as if her heart would burst from her chest. She could hardly wait to get these boxes packed and into the hands of children around the world.

≈

Josif folded the last circular table and rolled it into the fellowship hall closet. They'd finished filling the shoeboxes. Everyone had gone home, except Mirela, him, and the pastor who was now in his office, going over his sermon notes.

Josif watched Mirela. She was leaning across the counter, wiping up any remnants of the cookies the helpers had snacked on while they'd worked. She didn't look up at him, but she must have felt his eyes upon her because she smiled and said, "I think it went well."

"It went very well." He made his way to her, took the washcloth from her hand, and placed it in the sink. He wrapped his arms around her and pressed her close to him. "I'm so proud of you."

She didn't turn her face but talked into his shirt. "I think I was more nervous than I've ever been in my life."

Her chin tickled his chest and he pulled her away from him. Her brown eyes twinkled with merriment. He loved that her whole face lit up when she smiled. He touched her lips with the tip of his finger. He loved those lips. He wanted to claim them for his own.

Willing himself to wait, he grabbed her hand in his. "I have something I want to show you."

She pouted. "I thought you were going to kiss me."

"Oh, I will." He didn't look at her for fear his strength would dissolve and he'd end up wallowing her in kisses before he had the chance to talk with her. "Just not yet."

He dragged her out of the building and toward his car. Her church was the perfect setting for his plan. The small place of worship was nestled on a mountain. A small stream ran beside it, and just beyond the stream, the congregation had built a gazebo. The view from the gazebo was breathtaking. It overlooked a deep valley blanketed with a deep-green meadow. Red, orange, yellow, and salmon-colored leaves adorned the trees in preparation of winter. The white, purple, and yellow wildflowers that were scattered along the meadow had succumbed to their annual time of rest.

He stopped at his car to retrieve a wrapped shoebox. Mirela pointed at it. "What's that?"

"A present."

She placed her hand on her chest. "For me?"

"For you." He touched her nose and then grabbed her hand in his again. He guided her as they hopped over the stream, then up the few steps of the gazebo.

Mirela sucked in her breath. "Isn't this just one of the most amazing views in all the world?"

He agreed with her, but at the moment, he couldn't take his eyes off Mirela. His heartbeat quickened. They'd only officially been dating a month, but he felt he'd known her a lifetime. She tore her gaze from the mountains and looked down at the box. "You know I love shoebox presents."

Josif laughed, but his voice sounded too high. "Yes, I know you do."

He stared at her as he drank in the way the breeze blew her hair into her eyes, forcing her to keep pushing strands behind her ear. Her lips, the perfect shade of pink, drew him. She bit her bottom lip, and he glanced back up at her eyes.

She grinned. "So, you gonna let me open it?"

He laughed as he motioned for her to sit on the bench. "Yes, I am."

He handed her the box then he sat beside her. He'd expected her to find the seams of the wrapping and gently peel off the tape. Instead, Mirela ripped the paper to sheds, like a puppy mutilating a feather pillow. *I should have known she'd want to get it open quick.*

She lifted the lid, and it took all of his fortitude not to tear out the tissue paper and grab up the box. Instead he watched as she gingerly felt around until she found the small black box. She pulled it out and looked at him.

He took it from her grasp and kneeled down in front of her. Wrapping his hand around hers, he lifted her hand to his lips and kissed her palm. She stared down at him, her deep brown eyes wide with excitement.

He opened the box then removed the green opal ring. He held it between index finger and thumb. "Mama gave me this opal a few weeks ago. It's from our country. From Serbia."

Mirela leaned over and looked at the stone. She didn't speak as she placed her hand against her chest and tears welled in her eyes. With his free hand, he pulled a tissue out of his front pocket. He'd known she would cry.

"She told me I was to give this to my future wife."

Mirela gazed at him then dabbed her eyes with the tissue. Her chest rose and fell as she seemingly fought the need to let the tears rain down.

He took her left hand into his. "Mirela, this isn't a traditional engagement ring, but we are not a traditional couple." His tone lightened and he quipped, "Our parents arranged our marriage, and then we were separated for twenty-five years."

Mirela giggled as she sniffed and nodded at the same time.

"But God brought us back together."

Mirela gazed into his eyes. He could feel the love streaming from within them. Placing the ring on the tip of her finger, he said, "I love you, Mirela. Be my wife."

She pushed her finger through the ring then fell into him. "Of course I will. I love you."

He lost his balance and fell backward onto the gazebo floor. She toppled on top of him. She kissed his lips. "Of course, I'll marry you." She kissed him again. "What are you, crazy?" She kissed him a third time.

Josif tried to sit up, but Mirela kept planting kisses on him. Not that he minded, but he just didn't think it would look appropriate to be sprawled out in the gazebo with his girlfriend. *Fiancée.*

The realization that they were engaged washed over him as he stood and lifted her to her feet. Grabbing her face in both his hands, he claimed her lips. As she melted against him, he dug his hands into her long, soft hair. She'd said yes.

❧

The frigid Serbian air kissed Mirela's cheeks. Mound after mound of snow-capped mountains called to her, causing a deep yearning to trek through them, to learn more about the place she'd lived as a small girl. Members of their group had passed out every shoebox they'd brought. They'd read the Bible stories with the children. She'd laughed, cried, hugged, and played with them. It had been a blessed time for her. One she would always remember.

She sucked in a deep breath and peered up at the heavens. *And, God, Your Word never comes back void. May the children who made decisions for You be a witness to their friends and families. May Your word be spread in ways I could never imagine.*

From behind, a strong hand wrapped around her waist and pulled her close. Josif's warm breath danced across her cheek. "It's beautiful, isn't it?"

She swallowed. "More so than in pictures. More than I could remember."

"I'm glad you got to come to Serbia."

She turned to face him and wrapped her arms around his waist. "Someone made sure of it, didn't they?"

Josif furrowed his eyebrows and frowned, acting as if he had no idea what she was talking about. He'd made sure she had the funds to go Serbia. He'd even taken off from the hotel to go with her, as he'd wanted to see Serbia with her before they married. She smiled up at him then kissed his cheek. "Thank you, Josif."

The left side of his mouth curved up into a silly smile. "My life's been turned upside down since I met you."

"For the better, I hope."

He kissed her forehead. "You know it's been for the better. Much better." He pulled her closer and she nestled her cheek into his strong chest. "I'm sorry you didn't see your family."

A moment of pain sliced through her. She prayed she'd be able to see her sister and cousins, to witness to them. She'd hoped that maybe they'd already received Christ. But she hadn't met anyone who shared her sister's name, nor found anyone who knew of them. "God knows where they are."

"Yes, He does." Josif pulled away from their embrace and

pushed a strand of her always wayward hair away from her cheek. "And we were able to bless and share with so many children and families."

Mirela thought of the little blond girl who shared her name. She was two years older than Mirela had been when she received her shoebox but when the girl pulled a blond doll from her shoebox, the child's eyes had lit with a merriment that Mirela knew all too well. "This is an amazing ministry."

"I'd say. It even led me back to you. I'd have never known my future wife lived only forty-five minutes from me if she hadn't been preparing so many shoeboxes that they put her in the paper."

"And she wouldn't have been collecting shoeboxes if she hadn't felt such a burden to prepare them after having received one as a girl."

Josif's expression sobered. "We really have no idea how much God uses our obedience, do we?"

Mirela touched his stubbly cheek, noting how cute he looked with an unshaven face. Though she couldn't deny he was awfully cute with a shaven face as well. "I'm so thankful Mama Sesely read that article."

"I'm thankful you were collecting shoeboxes."

"Well, I'm thankful I received one so I could—" Before she could finish, Josif leaned down and pressed his lips against hers. She inwardly sighed. *Oh God, I'm so thankful.*

epilogue

Mirela looked down at the lace-fitted wedding gown she'd selected. She touched the small flower design stitched along the sweetheart neckline. She felt beautiful in the dress, and she knew Josif would love it.

Mirela had promised Josif she wouldn't tie her hair in knots, so the hairdresser had pinned up the sides and curled it so that big, soft ringlets fell all the way down her back.

"You look stunning."

Mirela turned at the sound of her sister's voice. Her mother and Ivy smiled at her. The light-green, tea-length bridesmaid's dresses Mirela had selected matched the green opal in her ring. "You look beautiful, Ivy."

Her mom allowed her fingers to trail the side of the veil. "Josif will be beside himself."

Mirela sucked in her breath. She hoped so. She wanted him to feel excitement and thrill and pride at his bride. She wanted him to be unable to take his eyes off her.

Her mother wrapped her arm around Mirela's. "It's time. Are you ready?"

She bit her bottom lip and nodded. They walked into the foyer of the small, country church. Originally she and Josif had wanted to invite only their families. And Cheryl since she'd become a Christian and they'd grown closer as the woman spent much of her time at Mirela's house, attending Bible study or just visiting. Of course, she'd invited Emily and Bella and Benny, even though Mirela knew Emily probably wouldn't show. But then her colleagues hinted they wanted to attend, and so did the hotel staff. And both their church families.

It soon got out of hand, and Mirela handed most of the planning over to her mother and Mama Sesely. She had no idea how many people would be scrunched into the small sanctuary, but she wouldn't care as long as Josif waited for her at the altar.

The music started and Mirela watched as Sofija and then Ivy started to walk down the aisle. She smiled down at Chloe who was practicing the motions of her walk as flower girl. Chloe started down the aisle, and Mirela's mom squeezed her arm.

Part of Mirela felt sad that her dad wasn't able to give her away, but she also felt thankful that her mom was there to do it as a sign of relinquishing her to God's plan. They'd grown even closer over the last few months, and Mirela knew God was working in her mother's heart to be able to fully trust Him with her daughters.

"Pomp and Circumstance" played from the piano at the front of the church. The foyer doors opened, and Mirela and her mom stepped into the aisle. Mirela's gaze locked with Josif's. He stood at the front of the sanctuary, handsome and ready in his black tuxedo.

The smile that spread his lips was contagious, and she found herself almost giddy as she began making her way down the long aisle to his side. He swiped his eyes with the back of his hand, and Mirela feared the overwhelming love in her heart would buckle her knees and she would melt into the carpet.

When she finally reached him, he mouthed the words, "I love you."

Longing for the pastor to hurry and ask her mother to give

her away, Mirela ached for Josif to take her hands in his. Her pastor's voice boomed. "Who gives this woman to this man?"

Her mother responded, "I do."

Mirela looked at her mom and saw the tears glistening in her eyes. Her mom lifted her veil over her head then placed a kiss on Mirela's cheek. She whispered, "I'm so happy for you."

"Thank you, Mom."

Mirela turned back to Josif. He took her hand in his, and it felt as if her body caught fire. She yearned to be his wife

The pastor's voice broke her thoughts. "Let us pray."

She bowed her head as the pastor led a prayer. When he finished, she looked up and noticed the centerpiece was not what she and her mom and Mama Sesely had planned—a large, circular arrangement of white roses with a few light green sprayed roses dotting it all around.

Instead, she saw a white box, the size of a shoebox. It was filled with flowers—pink, purple, yellow, white, but mainly green. Josif must have realized she was staring at it because he leaned over and whispered, "It was my idea."

She smiled at the man who would be her husband in only a few short minutes. The centerpiece was beautiful. It was perfect. A simple shoebox had meant so much to her as a girl who needed to know Jesus. God used it again to bring her to Josif. For her, a shoebox always brought the best of surprises.

A Letter To Our Readers

Dear Reader:

In order that we might better contribute to your reading enjoyment, we would appreciate your taking a few minutes to respond to the following questions. We welcome your comments and read each form and letter we receive. When completed, please return to the following:

Fiction Editor
Heartsong Presents
PO Box 719
Uhrichsville, Ohio 44683

1. Did you enjoy reading *Shoebox Surprise* by Jennifer Johnson?
   ❑ Very much! I would like to see more books by this author!
   ❑ Moderately. I would have enjoyed it more if

   _____
   _____
   _____

2. Are you a member of **Heartsong Presents**? ❑ Yes ❑ No
   If no, where did you purchase this book? _____
   _____

3. How would you rate, on a scale from 1 (poor) to 5 (superior), the cover design? _____

4. On a scale from 1 (poor) to 10 (superior), please rate the following elements.

   ____ Heroine   ____ Plot
   ____ Hero   ____ Inspirational theme
   ____ Setting   ____ Secondary characters

5. These characters were special because? _____

_____

_____

6. How has this book inspired your life? _____

_____

_____

7. What settings would you like to see covered in future
   Heartsong Presents books? _____

_____

_____

8. What are some inspirational themes you would like to see
   treated in future books? _____

_____

_____

9. Would you be interested in reading other **Heartsong
   Presents** titles? ❏ Yes ❏ No

10. Please check your age range:
     ❏ Under 18   ❏ 18-24
     ❏ 25-34   ❏ 35-45
     ❏ 46-55   ❏ Over 55

Name _____

Occupation _____

Address _____

City, State, Zip _____

E-mail _____

Heartsong

Presents

Great Inspirational Romance
at a Great Price!

Heartsong Presents books are inspirational romances in contemporary and historical settings, designed to give you an enjoyable, spirit-lifting reading experience. You can choose wonderfully written titles from some of today's best authors like Wanda E. Brunstetter, Mary Connealy, Susan Page Davis, Cathy Marie Hake, Joyce Livingston, and many others.

When ordering quantities less than six, above titles are $3.99 each.
Not all titles may be available at time of order.

HEARTSONG
PRESENTS

If you love Christian romance…

$12.⁹⁹

You'll love Heartsong Presents' inspiring and faith-filled romances by today's very best Christian authors…Wanda E. Brunstetter, Mary Connealy, Susan Page Davis, Cathy Marie Hake, and Joyce Livingston, to mention a few!

When you join Heartsong Presents, you'll enjoy four brand-new, mass-market, 176-page books—two contemporary and two historical—that will build you up in your faith when you discover God's role in every relationship you read about!

Mass Market 176 Pages

Imagine…four new romances every four weeks—with men and women like you who long to meet the one God has chosen as the love of their lives…all for the low price of $12.99 postpaid.

To join, simply visit www.heartsong presents.com or complete the coupon below and mail it to the address provided.

YES! Sign me up for Heartsong!

NEW MEMBERSHIPS WILL BE SHIPPED IMMEDIATELY!
Send no money now. We'll bill you only $12.99 postpaid with your first shipment of four books. Or for faster action, call 1-740-922-7280.

NAME_____

ADDRESS_____

CITY_____ STATE _____ ZIP _____

MAIL TO: HEARTSONG PRESENTS, P.O. Box 721, Uhrichsville, Ohio 44683
or sign up at WWW.HEARTSONGPRESENTS.COM